THE ORANOS IMPERATIVE

Published by Dark Titan Publishing. A division of Dark Titan Entertainment.

Also available in hardcover and eBook.

Dark Titan Universe is a branch of Dark Titan Entertainment.

First Printing 2021.

Hardcover ISBN: 978-1-7366984-1-9
Paperback ISBN: 978-1-7369944-2-9
eBook ISBN: 978-1-7366984-2-6

darktitanentertainment.com

WORKS BY TY'RON W. C. ROBINSON II

BOOKS/SHORT STORIES/PODCAST

DARK TITAN UNIVERSE SAGA

MAIN SERIES

Dark Titan Knights
The Resistance Protocol
Tales of the Scattered
Tales of the Numinous
Day of Octagon
Crossbreed
Heaven's Called
The Oranos Imperative

Forthcoming
Underworld
Magicks and Mysticism
The Resistance vs. The Enforcement Order

COLLECTIONS

Dark Titan Omnibus: Volume 1
Dark Titan Omnibus: Volume 2
Dark Titan One-Shot Collection

SPIN-OFFS

In A Glass of Dawn: The Casebook of Travis Vail
Maveth: Bloodsport
The Curse of The Mutant-Thing

Forthcoming
Trail of Vengeance
War of The Thunder Gods
Maveth vs. The Swordman

ONE-SHOTS

Maveth, The Death-Bringer
Mystery of The Mutant-Thing
Shade & Switchblade
Retribution of Cain
The Mythologists
Ambush Bot
Kang-Zhu

THE HAUNTED CITY SAGA

The Legendary Warslinger: The Haunted City I
Battle of Astolat: A Haunted City Prequel (KOBO Exclusive)
Redemption of the Lost: The Haunted City II
Consequences of the Suffering: The Haunted City III (Forthcoming)
The Haunted City Collection

SYMBOLUM VENATORES

Symbolum Venatores: The Gabriel Kane Collection
Hod: A Symbolum Venatores Book
Symbolum Venatores: War of The Two Kingdoms
Symbolum Venatores: Elrad's Chronicles
Symbolum Venatores: Mystery of the Magician (Forthcoming)
Symbolum Venatores: Twilight of the Gods (Forthcoming)
Symbolum Venatores Collection

EVERWAR UNIVERSE
EverWar Universe: Knights & Lords
EverWar Universe: The Damned Ones (Forthcoming)

FRIGHTENED!
Frightened!: The Beginning
Frightened!: The Light Sky (Forthcoming)

INSTINCTS
Lost in Shadows: Remastered
Snadow in a Mirror: Instincts II (Forthcoming)

DARK TITAN'S THE DEAD DAYS
Accounts of The Dead Days
Brand New Day: The Dead Days I (Forthcoming)

PRODIGIOUS WORLDS
Mark Porter of Argoron (Forthcoming)
Raiders of Vanok (Forthcoming)
Praxus of Lithonia (Forthcoming)

CHEVAH MYTHOS
The Eleventh Hour: A Chevah Mythos Story

THE HORDE
The Horde
The Dreaded Ones (Forthcoming)

OTHER BOOKS
The Book of The Elect
The Extended Age Omnibus

THE DARK TITAN AUDIO EXPERIENCE PODCAST
Season 1: Introductions
Season 2: In a Glass of Dawn
Season 2.5: Accounts of The Dead Days
Season 3: Battle For Astolat
Season 4: Hallow Sword: Cursed

THE ORANOS IMPERATIVE

TY'RON W. C. ROBINSON II

CONTENTS

HALLOW SWORD: TIME FOR CHANCE

I

WELCOME TO RETROPOLIS

A snowy day in Retropolis and the Mayor is greeted with a newcomer to the city. The visitor walked into the Mayor's office, greeting him as he sat down near the desk. The Mayor sat before him and the visitor slid over a folder. The Mayor looked with confusion as he opened the folder. He saw what was inside and nodded with a grin.

"You honestly believe this is all it takes to get where you want to go?"

"Hear me out, Mr. Mayor. I'm just seeking to make this city better. From what I've been told about this place, there aren't a lot of people like me. Both in mind and spirit."

"You think you can do a better job than the officials we already have?"

"I know I can. The criminals will be put to a stop immediately. New restrictions will be made to keep them in check. Very simple."

"And what of The Swordman figure?"

"Come on." The visitor chuckled." You don't think he's real do you?"

"In such a short time, this city has seen things that would make even an unbeliever shake in their boots."

"So, the whole invasion thing? The Battle of Retropolis? That was all real? Not some typical terrorist bullshit?"

"Very real."

"So, this Swordman guy, he's real? Very real?"

"Yes he is."

"And those others who were seen with him are real as well?"

"Haven't you seen the videos, Mr. Hunt?" The Mayor asked.

"I don't watch a lot of stuff, I'm afraid. Work gets the most of me."

"I understand. A man such as yourself takes your job seriously. Well then, show me what you can do to make this city safer."

"I will."

Mr. Hunt stood up from the seat, greeting the Mayor before taking his leave. Once outside of City Hall, he is surrounded by the media. All clamoring for his answers to make Retropolis a better place. Hunt glanced up beyond the reporters and saw the cameras coming from the vans and trucks. He sighed.

Kenari sat in the Swordlair, watching the live news with Hunt. Behind Kenari walked in Allison, who placed her arm around him as they were both focused on the news. Kenari watched as Hunt stated the city was in need of some dire changes and it could no longer allow criminals such as Death, Sir Onyx, or J to continue thriving. Hunt said he will bring forth a better Retropolis and he told the citizens of the city to remember the name of Harold Hunt. Kenari scoffed as he turned off the TV.

"What do you make of the man?" Allison asked.

"He's persistent. I can already tell. Determined. That I see."

"Are you planning on meeting him?"

"Meeting him as who?" Kenari asked. "Why would he want to see Kenari Clark. He'll assuredly desire to have a talk with The Swordman."

Kenari walked toward the closet, turning the knob and the closet opened, unveiling the Swordsuit and the sword standing in front. Kenari stared in the eyes of the mask for several seconds before making a decision.

"We'll see what he makes of it."

As the night had come in, police reported sightings of Cartavious Cage roaming around the city neighborhoods. Cage was lurking around homes, seeking which one to break in. Cage had been released from Pegasus Prison after he proclaimed of being visited by strange dark figure who entered his cell from the wall. Cartavious lurked in the bushes around the homes. He heard something hit the ground behind him and turned with his knife. He swiped the knife and it glistened over The Swordman's chest-plated armor.

"Why are you out here, Cage?"

"Because I have business to attend to. Go somewhere else and bother another."

"You're done for the night."

"Says who?"

"Me."

Cage lunged at Swordman with the knife. Swordman dodged to his left and slammed his elbow across Cage's wrist, dropping the knife into the dirt. Swordman snatched Cage by his throat and heat butted him into unconsciousness. Afterwards, Swordman gathered Cage and took him to Rockward. The police arrived at the scene just as the Swordman left the scene in the Land-Dagger. While driving, Swordman spotted several men walking down the street. They were all dressed in suits. Very business-like apparel. They waved at Swordman, getting his attention. He decided to stop and slowly exited the vehicle, staring at the men. There were twelve in total.

"What do you want?"

"We seek Harold Hunt."

"What makes you think I know where he is?"

"We only seek an audience with him. Nothing more."

"For what cause?"

"We're attorneys and our boss wants to talk to him."

"Then tell your boss to find him yourself and quit lurking on the streets at this time of night. Otherwise, I would suspect you to be the wicked doers like such others."

"You don't have to worry about us, good sir. We're all good people."

"There is no good people. Now return to your residences and leave the streets. If not, I'll stop you all myself."

The Swordman returned to his vehicle and drove away as the attorneys left the area. While Swordman returned to his estate, he thought to himself concerning the attorneys. Their speech and their place in the streets. He wondered who were they and why were they seeking Harold Hunt.

II

<u>SHARP OPPORTUNITIES</u>

The morning after, Hunt arrived at City Hall and held a conference for all citizens of Retropolis to attend. Many came to hear him speak while others watched in their homes. Kenari and Allison watched the conference from the Swordlair. Mayor Baker watched from his office, even though the conference is being held just outside. Hunt was determined and adamant on his choices of actions regarding the city.

"Mr. Hunt." A reporter said. "What would be your take on the actions of The Swordman?"

"His actions you ask? Well, for starters, I would like to meet this living myth myself. See how his mind works. Perhaps, he might understand my motives more than you all. However, when it comes to his acts of justice, I do not recommend he kill those who are in his way. Even though, according to the Retropolis police, this Swordman has only killed thugs attached to such crime lords like Onyx or J. I have to respect that."

"What if he doesn't comply with your guidelines for the city?"

Hunt sighed. He thought for a second, returning his focus toward the audience.

"Then measures must be taken. Whatever the case may be."

Hunt held his hands up, ending the conference as he walked away being followed in mass by reporters and civilians with more questions. Kenari turned off the TV and went to his desk, working on his equipment, particularly the wrist grappler. Allison entered the lair, seeing her husband at the desk. She glanced at the TV and back toward Kenari.

"So, how did the conference go?"

"He seems like he wants to do the right thing. I get that."

"But?"

"But our paths may not be on the same path. He told the people if my actins do not go along with his rules, there would be measures."

"Well, he's new to this land. If he only heard the stories of The Swordman and his responses to those who've sought him out in violence or petty threats."

"He wants to meet me. I want to meet him. Not sure how or where."

"Only way that would happen was if he was kidnapped or something. Or he could find a way to bring you out. You don't have a signal, you know."

"Why would I need one?"

"No reason. Just a thought."

Kenari nodded with a grin as Allison left the lair.

Later in the day, Hunt returned to the Mayor's office and sat with him in his office. The two talked about the conference and the Mayor was impressed with Hunt's public speaking, to which Hunt gave gratitude toward his teachers in English class. The Mayor stood up from his seat and shook Hunt's hand, fully welcoming him to the city of Retropolis. Hunt smiled and the two drank wine to celebrate.

Sometime past the afternoon as Hunt was preparing to head back to his home, he was greeted by the twelve attorneys at the steps of City Hall. Hunt paused himself, looking at the well-dressed men. He nodded and stepped forward.

"I'm sorry, but the conference was hours ago. If you wish to speak to me, save it for tomorrow please."

"We do not wish to speak with you, Mr. Hunt."

"Then, why are you coming to me as if you have something to say?"

"Our boss wants to talk to you. Says you and he have many things in common."

"Well. First off, I'm flattered. Your boss has good taste. Second, tell your boss if he wants to have a word with me, set it up for tomorrow. I'll have enough time then."

"We cannot."

"Pardon."

"I said we cannot."

The attorneys began ambushing Hunt. Not harming him physically, but they dragged him to a nearby van and tossed him inside as they all jumped in and the van drove from the City Hall. Several civilians were nearing the location and had witnessed the event. Many ran away, some were confused. Only one had contacted the police concerning the scene. Once news had spread across Retropolis of Hunt's kidnapping, The Swordman was already out scouting the city for him. He searched and eventually tracked down the van at an abandoned building.

"The old courthouse." The Swordman said. "Why bring him here?"

Inside the old courthouse, the Attorneys brought Hunt into the courtroom where they placed him in a chair and stood to the side. Hunt looked around in the dim-lit room. Confused and uncertain of his place.

"What's going on here? Why kidnap me?"

"Because, I want to speak with you." said a figure in the shadow.

Hunt tried to look closer, but the figure approached him with a lamp. Presenting himself before Hunt. The figure was dressed in a dark blue suit with a fedora.

"Who are you supposed to be?" Hunt asked.

"Call me Mr. Harvey Madison. I'm a lawyer. A very damn good one."

"Ok. So, why send your puppets to kidnap me?"

"Because I needed to speak to you about your ideas for this city. I have some suggestions in mind."

"I'm not looking for suggestions. What I have, I have. Nothing more."

The lawyer laughed.

"Give it time, Mr. Hunt. Soon, you will understand what this city does to its inhabitants."

"Let me go and you'll find out what comes next."

"I think not."

The sound of shattering glass echoed through the room with moonlight shining through. The Attorneys gazed up as did the Lawyer and Hunt. From the area where the glass was located moved a quickening shadow which began taking out the Attorneys in he dark. Hunt could only see glimpses of the shadow as the Attorneys collapsed to the floor. The Lawyer stepped back from the area and ran toward the wall, turning on the lights. Once the lights shined, he saw his Attorneys on the ground with The Swordman standing over them.

"Ah. I knew you would show up."

"For a reason." The Swordman said. "I'm taking Hunt out of here."

"I don't think so. You'll be too preoccupied."

"You won't be much to handle."

"I wasn't talking about me."

Curious about his words, Swordman turned toward Hunt and a foot appeared out of nowhere, kicking Swordman in the chest, shoving him back from Hunt. Swordman looked up and saw a figure dressed in orange armor covering its body with a mask featuring two red eye slits. The Swordman clenched his fists and walked forward.

"Who are you?"

"I'm the guy who the Lawyer called up. Just in case you showed up."

"Well, here I am."

The Swordman and the armored figure lunged toward each other with fists in front.

III

<u>DUE TO LAW</u>

The Swordman kicked the figure across the room. The Lawyer stood back with his eyes going from the fight to Hunt in the chair. Hunt struggled to free himself from the seat as Swordman fought the armored figure behind him. Only hearing the grunts and impacts to the floor. The Swordman grabbed the figure by the throat and slammed him into the ground before the figure kicked himself up to his feet.

"Who are you?" Swordman asked.

"Well, might as well introduce myself properly."

The figure held out his arms and from his fingers pierced out sharp silver claws. Swordman stood firm with his fists prepared as the figure started scratching the wall near him.

"Codename's Clawmaster."

Clawmaster rushed toward Swordman, swiping away. The Swordman blocked the claws with his forearm armor, he kicked Clawmaster in the knee before grabbing his head with his arm and tossing him near the Lawyer.

"Seems your codename doesn't instill much fear as you hoped." Swordman mentioned.

"I wasn't going for fear. Scare tactics aren't my thing."

Clawmaster jumped and slammed his claws into Swordman's forearm, kicking him in the abdomen before shoving him back from Hunt. Swordman sighed and pulled out his sword, to which Clawmaster was intrigued. He glanced at his claws and to the sword.

"I wonder how sharp that blade is."

"Come and find out."

Clawmaster slashed and swiped against the sword as Swordman held still. Twirling the blade into every slice from Clawmaster's hands. The Lawyer began to worry as Hunt turned himself around to see Swordman deflecting the blows from Clawmaster. Each blow became slower and slower as Clawmaster's breath was increasing. Swordman paused as Clawmaster's next attack hit the sword, breaking three of the claws from his right hand. Stunned. He glanced at his hand and back to the sword before The Swordman punched and kicked him in the head. Clawmaster fell to the floor, unconsciousness. The Lawyer gasped and ran for the door, yet, Swordman used his wrist grappler to snatch Lawyer's hand from the doorknob and pulled him closer and gave him a punch of his own. The Swordman sheath his blade and freed Hunt from the seat.

"Thanks." Hunt said.

"You wanted to speak with me."

"Ah. Yeah. How about right after we get these two behind bars, eh."

The police were called with Commissioner Austin and Detectives Justine Copeland and Cash Hankinson arriving at the scene. Justine grabbed Lawyer, placing him in handcuffs.

"I don't know where you came from, but you're surely like the others." Justice uttered.

"Oh, my dear. I want to speak to my attorneys." The Lawyer said.

"Not happening anytime soon." Austin added as Justine escorted him out.

"Oh, Commissioner, we haven't had the chance to meet."

Hunt said, extending his hand.

"You're that new guy."

"I am. Harold Hunt."

Austin greeted Hunt with a handshake and a smile.

"I know I'm late at this but, welcome to Retropolis."

Hunt sighed and turned around, seeing The Swordman was gone. Austin nodded with a grin, looking at Hunt's confusion.

"He was just here."

"It happens in this city, Mr. Hunt. Like nature."

The following day, Hunt spoke to the citizens of Retropolis about his kidnapping and The Swordman's rescue. He thanked him for the save and stated he will look into way of allowing someone of his caliber, pearly the risen heroes, a way at protecting the city without the harm of law enforcement interference. Elsewhere, the Lawyer was placed into Pegasus Prison after his arrest when claims came out of him going mad. Clawmaster was stripped of his armor, revealing himself to be Antonio Jameson, a mercenary who moves throughout Canada for his work, was taken to Rockward Penitentiary. The city has now began calling Harvey Madison the Mad Lawyer.

CHOSEN SON: YOU'VE CROSSED THE LINE

I

<u>WHO IS POWERFUL?</u>

On a bright sunny day in Enigma City, the people go about their business. Until the ground began to tremble. Startling the people, they looked to one another in confusion. The quaking continued and from beneath the roads burst out a figure made of molten lava. A humanoid figure. Its eyes surging with magma as were its hands and feet. Every step it took, it melted the concrete. The entity began conjuring balls of magma and tossing them into the buildings and vehicles. The people fled in panic as the entity let out a loud screeching roar. The roar echoed throughout the city and further. Tiny hints of the roar had reached the Fortress of Cytron and inside was darkness. Except for the glowing lightning eyes of Taltus, who bolted from the fortress, heading straight for Enigma City.

The volcanic entity continued its attack as Taltus bolted down from the sky towards the entity, striking it with a punch, knocking it far across the city. Taltus followed the debris of ash on the roads and found the entity pulling itself from underneath the rubble.

"Who are you?" Taltus asked.

"I go by many names of the earth's minerals. Folktales only call me Volcanca."

Volcanca attacked Taltus with similar blows of his own. Taltus went into a building behind, holding his chest from the attack. Feeling Volcanca's strength, he just as strong. Taltus returned the blow with several punches and a tackle through the city streets. Passing the civilians in such speed, they only caught the glimpse of his blue cape. Taltus reached the end of the city and threw Volcanca out of the city limits. Volcanca stood up, conjuring more magma blows and throwing them toward the titagod. Taltus reflected them with his lightning vision and used it on Volcanca's chest to slow the entity down.

"I will not fall!" Volcanca yelled, blasting a magma beam.

Taltus dodged the coming lava and rushed toward Volcanca, grabbing the entity by the face and slamming it into the ground continually until the magma ceased from its hands. Taltus removed his hand from Volcanca's face, seeing how the magma left a mark on his hand. He wiped the scorches off his hand and turned around toward the city. What Taltus saw were the civilians cheering him on as well as four peculiar figures. They did not cheer nor boo. They only watched and they watched closely. Taltus looked closer and cold sense power surging from each of them. When he took a step forward, they vanished into thin smoke. Not even the civilians could tell who they were or where they came from. Taltus sighed and returned his focus toward Volcanca, taking the entity to a newly built prison which stood a distance afar from Enigma City. The name of the prison was never given to the public.

Sometime later, Taltus returned to the fortress to heal himself of the scorched burn and to find a way to track down the power source he sensed from the four figures.

II

<u>WHO ARE THE NOBLE FORCE?</u>

While Stephanie Vale worked in her office during the day, she gazed over to the window to see Taltus hovering. Startling her, she dropped her pen and papers, causing several of the other reporters outside of her office to look. They stare and she shook it off. Waving them away.

"It's nothing. Just an accident. That's all."

The other reporters returned to their business as Stephanie approached the window with caution. She waved her hands around, though Taltus did not understand what they meant. Stephanie sighed, pointing up. Taltus understood and flew above the building. Stephanie left her office and went to the top of the building, where Taltus was waiting. She approached him nervously.

"I have to ask, I thought we would never get the chance to talk."

"Now we can. On an important cause."

"What cause?"

"During the fight with Volcanca, I noticed four distinct figures watching alongside the civilians. They were infused with powers beyond mortals. I cannot track them from Cytron, but you can."

"And how can I do that?"

"You tracked down all the sources to discover me, didn't you."

"Um. Yes. Yes I did. For a good cause."

"I understand. I know I haven't been as open to the world as many had hoped. I appear to be somewhat distant to your kind. But, that is not my true calling. Many have said I am their savior. A beacon of hope. Someone to aspire to. I do not understand such thoughts. Perhaps, I will come to learn them in time."

"It takes time. Trust me." Stephanie said with a smile. "Just one step at a time is all."

Taltus nodded.

"Now, what is it you wanted me to do involving these figures?"

"I need you to track them down. Find out where they might be. Once you do, I'll meet with them. Someone of my stature must before they expose themselves to the general public."

"I got you. So, when I gather the evidence you need, do you find me or do I find you?"

"I'll find you." Taltus said. "Besides, you already know where I am."

Taltus turned away and flew off with Stephanie only watching on. She sighed and returned to her office. Throughout the day, Stephanie search through many files which were on the public record. She found nothing. Unsure of where answer could be, she looked around and thought for a moment, coming across graffiti of the T.I.T.A.N. symbol under a nearby bridge within Enigma City.

"Maybe." She said.

Stephanie tracked down the closets T.I.T.A.N. base she could, eventually discovering one just on the outskirts of Enigma City. Their place of being there was due to the *Battle of Retropolis* event not taking place in Enigma, repeating another disastrous scenario. Stephanie arrived at the base, seeing the large gate in front. She exited her vehicle as T.I.T.A.N. agents stood before her on the other side.

"Who are you?" An agent asked.

"I'm Stephanie Vale. I'm a reporter."

"Reporters aren't welcomed here."

"But, it's urgent. Taltus told me to search for something important. I'm sure you guys might know what I'm looking for."

"How can we be sure of this?"

"Because," A voice said from behind the agents. "I'm familiar with her work."

The agents turned around, seeing Colonel Evan Nader approaching them. He nodded as they lowered their firearms and opened the gate Stephanie entered, greeting Nader.

"You know of me?"

"Not only because of Taltus, but your work in discovering him actually aided us."

"My work helped you guys?"

"Sure did. Although, we were close to finding him. Just you gave us some pointers to use. Good work."

"Well, thank you."

"No. Thank you."

Stephanie followed Nader into the base, where she saw many agents and scientists working. She was never in a place such as this. Questions rambled in her mind. What to say and how to say it. Nader noticed her twitching eyes toward the scientists as some were moving around material from the Retropolis battle.

"You can ask." Nader said. "We don't bite."

"Um. Does the government know you're harboring extraterrestrial material?"

"First, its inter-dimensional material, not extraterrestrial. Second, which government?"

"The American Government."

"I don't see why it would be their concern. Besides, the material was in Retropolis. Dropped on Canadian soil."

Stephanie scoffed.

"I see now. I'm surprised no one has said anything about it being here."

"Because we only give out trust to those worthy of the word. Otherwise, we'll have to remove such traitors from the cause."

"And you've done that before."

"Once or twice." Nader nodded. "Now, this way, Ms. Vale."

Nader entered an office room, loaded with files. Stephanie entered and was quickly impressed. Each file was categorized in its proper place. No errors in her sight. Nader knew she would approve of such detail. She turned over to one section in the office and found a section labeled "Risen Heroes" with two distinct differences. One slot was labeled, "Discovered" and the other, "Undiscovered."

"Wait, so there are more of them out there?"

"Yeah. We've only been able to track down the slight movements. Abilities and suchlike."

"And how many are there so far?"

"Too many to keep count in a day. It's like the earth was preparing to let these people out."

"Well, that is why I'm here."

"Is that right? What are you looking for exactly?"

"Taltus told me of four individuals he saw in Enigma City. He said he couldn't make them out, but could only sense their power. They were peculiar."

"Four." Nader said. "I think I know who you're looking for."

Nader walked over to the Undiscovered slot and pulled out a folder. He handed it to Stephanie and as she opened it, she saw four individuals. Their details and their location. She nodded."

"This must be them."

"Why is Taltus interested in finding these folks?"

"He wants to know who they are and why they were in the city that day. Wants to protect them from the wrong exposure."

"You can't protect anyone from wrong exposure. It's going to come one way or another. They just have to make a choice when it comes."

"I'll tell him that. You don't mind if I take this, do you?"

"Just make sure to bring it back in one piece. Either you or Taltus. Your choice."

"It could be him. He's faster than I am."

"And yet, not as clever." Nader grinned.

Stephanie exited the base and returned to Enigma City. She drove further out to the Fortress of Cytron and before she could exit her vehicle, Taltus was already standing at the door. She shook her head with a sigh.

"Always that quick."

"Depends. I'm assuming you're here because you found something."

"I did." Stephanie handed him the folder.

"There are the ones I saw?" Taltus asked, examining the four files.

"You tell me. Those were the only one I was able to come across. Thanks to Evan Nader, of course."

"Nader? You mean he knew about them?"

"He knows a lot. Although, said I helped them out."

"With what?"

"Discovering you."

Taltus looked and only smiled before returning the folder to Stephanie.

"I have what I need."

"So, what's your next move?"

"I'm going oversees for a bit. Meet these guys and see what will come of it."

Taltus took off into the air with the blast of a sonic boom.

Stephanie smiled as she returned to her vehicle and drove away.

III

<u>WHO IS GOOD?</u>

Taltus flew over the Atlantic Ocean, coming over the country of England. Taltus arrived in Blackpool and while he flew, he began sensing the same energy around him. He paused himself and hovered still. His eyes closed as he increased his hearing and energy senses. Without haste, Taltus opened his eyes and saw the four figures below him atop a building. Taltus hovered down before them and saw them in full. They were not afraid of him, only curious.

"I've been looking for you four."

"We know." Said the one in front. "We've been wanting to talk with you."

"Then, why didn't you say anything back in Enigma City and how did you get all the way over here within such short time?"

"Teleportation is my thing, lad. Pardon my manners, I am Dusk. Aristocratic Dusk. My colleagues are Archduke, Peer, and Rosalind. Together, we are called the Noble Force."

"Noble Force, you say. Good to meet all of you. I can sense your abilities. Each of you. I can see you're very powerful."

"Powerful?" Dusk scoffed. "I thought you would toss us with the others out there. We do what needs to be done on these parts. Such as yourself and the others in the States."

"Why were you in Enigma City that day anyway?"

"Honestly, we wanted to see you in battle. Listen, *Talts*, we heard about the Battle of Retropolis. Hell, the world knows of it. Your existence is widely know and only those in the States can get a glimpse at your might. Besides those lucky Canadians in Retropolis."

"I understand your enthusiasm, however, I did not become who I am simply for fame or fortune. I do what I can to protect the innocent from idols. Idols who would use them as puppets for their own pleasures and glory."

"Sound like you're a good man." Dusk nodded. "Shame the world's gone the opposite direction."

"I am what I was raised to be. A man of justice and truth. Even if I have to stand alone."

Dusk turned to his colleagues and they agreed with him. Dusk shrugged his shoulders.

"Then, we have something to ask of you."

"And what may that be?"

"Teach us these ways of justice and truth. Perhaps, with your aid, we can achieve the same things here in England. Otherwise, we'll have to just use alternative ways."

"Alternative as in?"

"Kill them simply."

"Killing criminals or innocents?"

"Which ever one caused the crime. It's not always the answer to you and your kind. But, the thing is, this is England. This is Blackpool. Our turf. Sometimes, vengeance gets the job done and it brings fear over the people. They've learned to respect us."

"You mean fear you."

"Eh. A compliment."

"Alright then. Where do we start?"

"You tell me." Dusk replied. "You're the one with the super-hearing. I'm sure you'll be able to catch a crime going on before the four of us notice."

Taltus hovered above them into the air and listened to the

surroundings. He could hear all of what was happening in Blackpool. Vehicles honking, bells ringing, people speaking. In one instance, Taltus caught the sound of a gun cocking. His eyes opened.

"That way." Taltus pointed.

"Lead the way." Dusk said.

Taltus flew forward as the Noble Force followed. Dusk conjured a force field, giving him levitation. Rosalind flew in similar fashion to Taltus whereas Archduke leaped, and Peer twirled his staff to hover. Upon their arrival, they saw a gang of armed criminals attempting to break into a military base. Dusk's eyes grew dark and Taltus saw it. His eyes were almost solid black.

"I take it you know them." Taltus said.

"I do. These bastards call themselves the WatchGang. They prance around England taking military weaponry and using it against the people. I've seen the work first-hand."

"Sure, you handled it well."

"Archduke smashed them into the pavement. It's what he wanted to do."

Taltus turned to Archduke, he was silent and still. Face stern with his eyes locked on the WatchGang.

"Now, I have a plan." Taltus said.

"What kind of plan?"

"I'll swoop in and distract them. That way, you and your colleagues can intercept their weapons and take them out. One shot is all that's needed. Nothing else. Nothing more."

"What if they fight back?" Peer asked.

"Or shoot us?" Rosalind mentioned.

"Same rule applies. No killing."

"Didn't you kill that gargoyle dragon thing back home?" Dusk referenced.

"I did not. It still lives. Just in a secure prison."

"What if he gets out again?"

"He'll face the same circumstances as the first time. Now, we need to focus on this gang. Ready?"

"Make your move." Dusk smirked.

Taltus nodded and flew with great speed toward the WatchGang. Within a second, they were startled by the sudden gust of wind. They circled around. Nearly a dozen of them with their firearms pointed to the sky.

"What was that?!" One asked.

"I don't know. That's not normal around here!"

Taltus rushed pass them once more, startling them again as a few of them slipped and fell. Taltus flew back to Dusk and nodded.

"Your turn."

Dusk and the Force moved down the hill toward the WatchGang. Getting their attention, the Gang fired the rounds toward them. Dusk dodged the bullets and knocking several of them away with his force field.

"Get that grass-headed one!"

One of the men said firing his rounds toward Rosalind, who flew over him and twirled in the air to pass through the bullets. Peer twirled his staff to deflect the bullets, and Archduke stood still as the rounds didn't pierce his skin or clothing. Taltus watched on. Studying the young team. He felt they were powerful, now he's witnessing it. Dusk used his force field to knock the rifle from the gang member's hand and grabbed him by his throat. His eyes turning dark. Taltus spotted it and flew down toward them. Rosalind, Peer, and Archduke quickly defeated the others while Dusk taunting the one in his grasp.

"You have him." Taltus said.

"Yeah. But, I what cost will it bring forth later? He'll come back with his blokes and do it all over again."

"Not if he faces true justice. Do not kill him."

Dusk sighed. Staring into the eyes of the gang member.

"You know something, Talts, you speak of true justice. But, do you even know the truth of the word?"

"What are you saying?"

"What I am saying is the justice you speak of, it doesn't work anymore. Not in a world where there's guys like him and guys like us. It's a melting pot boiling over until there's nothing left."

"It will not boil over unless we make a stand. To keep things in their proper place."

"Proper place? And that is what? Guys like him behind cell doors only to be let out in a matter of three to five years? That's not enough."

"You talk a lot." The gang member said toward Dusk. "Listen to the big guy and let me go. Otherwise, finish me."

"Don't listen to him, Dusk. He's trying to rile you up."

"Yeah. That's what I'm doing. Getting under your skin aren't I? shame. That makes you weak if I can do that when you have such power and I only carry a gun."

"Shut up."

"Or what? You'll kill me?" The gang member chuckled. "Do your worst."

"Don't kill him." Taltus said. "Take him to the police. Let them deal with him."

Dusk shook. His hands trembling and his eyes completely dark.

"I... I can't do that, Talts."

"Quit being a bitch and take me out!" The gang member yelled.

"Don't!" Taltus screamed as Dusk placed his hand over the gang member's face and with his power snatched the gang member's head from his body.

"Why?' Taltus said. "Why did you kill him?"

"Because, that's the thing about us. Noble Force. We can't simply let the guilty move on freely with their lives after taking another. It's not in us."

"I cannot allow the four of you to continue this kind of justice as you call it."

"No. It's not justice we're after, it's vengeance. And only vengeance gets shit done."

"Then, I have to put you in your proper places. That way, you'll know how to operate in this world. To navigate freely and do you duty."

"Ah, shut up with the talk. I'm done talking and you're in our way of our justice."

"I will not allow either of you to walk freely after this."

"That's too bad." Dusk smirked.

Archduke rammed Taltus into the military base wall and started pummeling him with punches. Taltus blocked the blows with his forearms. Peer ran over and slammed the staff atop Taltus, leaving no effect. Rosalind extended her hands as the weeds from underneath the concrete rose up and snatched Taltus by his arms and legs.

"You see, we're only doing our job. Your ways are old school, Talts. We're the new school. This world will know our ways and they will follow suit."

"I cannot allow that." Taltus replied, snapping the weeds and hovering above them.

"So, it's a fight you want?" Dusk asked.

"Not a fight. A lesson."

"We're waiting!" Dusk screamed.

IV

<u>WHO IS NOBLE?</u>

Taltus fired his lightning vision toward the ground in front of the Force, stopping them in their steps. Dusk chuckled as the electricity sparked in front oh him. He stared at Taltus, seeing his eyes glowing with lighting sparking from them. Dusk clapped his hands and nodded.

"You got some feats on you, lad! Too bad, there's more of us!"

"I don't want to hurt you. Any of you."

"That's the only way you'll put a stop to us, you self-righteous prick!"

Archduke leaped into the air, spearing Taltus into the military base. Their brawl reached the city of Blackpool, where the news had begun to capture it on camera. The news spread throughout the world, where even Stephanie and Alex were witnessing it back in Enigma City. Archduke went for a punch, Taltus blocked his fist and kicked him into the air with both his feet, flying up to catch Archduke. He grabbed him by his torso and tossed him into the pavement. Archduke rose up, shaking himself as Taltus fell on him with his weight. Dusk, Peer, and Rosalind arrived as Archduke was knocked out and Taltus walked through the flowing debris, staring at them. Civilians fled the area as the two opposing forces stared one another in the street.

"One down. Three more."

"You killed him!" Dusk yelled.

"I did not. He's only sleeping. He'll wake up in a few hours behind bars. As will the rest of you."

Dusk grunted and stomped his feet. His anger was kindling in him as he eyes grew dark as the night sky. Peer twirled his staff as Rosalind lifted herself with the weeds and vines from the ground. Taltus hovered. Only staring as his cape flowed with the wind.

"Take this son of a bitch down!" Dusk screamed.

The Force collectivity attacked Taltus with their abilities. The attacks did no harm to the titagod. He stumbled after a sudden blow from Peer's staff. Taltus grabbed the staff, snapping it in half. Peer froze in place as Taltus punch him to the ground. Rosalind conjured several vines, wrapping them around Taltus' arms and neck. She squeezed his neck as he hovered closer toward them with Dusk throwing shadow discs at Taltus' chest.

"Something's got to give with this guy!" Dusk yelled.

"He's powerful." Rosalind replied. "Maybe too powerful."

"No! We're the Noble Force! We're the future of heroes! We can overpower him!"

Rosalind held the weeds and vines as much as she could. Struggling to hold Taltus in place. He grabbed the vines with his hands, pulling Rosalind toward him. Taltus caught her by the throat, holding her up as she gasped for breath. She let out a exhale of breath as Taltus dropped her to the ground. Dusk only stared in disbelief. Taltus showed no emotion, just focus.

"Before you ask, she is not dead. Neither is Peer. This is your last chance to give up, Dusk."

Dusk looked around at the buildings, seeing several civilians stayed behind to watch the fight. He grinned, using his force field ability to grab several civilians, holding them hostage in an energy field. Taltus stepped forward.

"Stop right there!" Dusk said. "You care for these blokes, I see."

"Because they're innocent. Let them go."

"Or what?!"

Taltus sighed, shaking his head in shame.

"You leave me no choice."

Taltus focused his eyes and unleashed the lightning vision again, only this time, the electricity struck Dusk in his head and chest. Dusk twitched as he was being electrocuted, losing his grip on the force field and setting the civilians free. They ran away as Taltus stopped and Dusk fell to his knees, gasping for breath. Taltus walked toward him. Dusk looked, holding his hands up.

"Alright, alright!" Dusk said. "I give. I give."

"Do you?" Taltus questioned.

Dusk showed a sinister smirk and stretch forth his hands toward Taltus. Yet, nothing happened. He did it again. No effect. Dusk looked at his hands with questions rambling his mind.

"What did you do to me?!"

"My lightning vision not only shocked you, but sparked a light within you, burning out the darkness you kept buried. it's a fitting revelation now. You were powered by your anger, your rage, your depression. It only needed to be spark to be purged. You no longer can control the shadows, Dusk. You're finished."

"No. I am not finished! I will have my vengeance!"

"That's the problem, you seek vengeance. Only with hope does one achieve what you seek. Hope is what empowers us to continue. To keep fighting. No matter the consequences that we face."

Taltus gazed up to see a news cameraman aimed at him. On the screens across the world was Taltus giving the words he spoke. They began to inspire the people. Taltus nodded to the news crew as he took Dusk and the Force to the same secure prison where the Dragon Gargoyle is kept. That prison is only referred to in name as *Awides*.

Taltus returned to Enigma City and was immediately hailed as the protector and savior of the city. He later discovered through Stephanie's connection that the world sought him for his abilities. They saw him as a true hero the world could aspire to. Taltus, knowing he was uncertain to be a hero to the people took it upon himself to declare that no innocents would be harmed or treated wrong while he resides in the world among them.

I

<u>WHAT COMES NEXT</u>

During the midday in Newark, New Jersey, Nathan Hawke sat in his office talking with Alice Jacobs and Ricky Carter about their adventures out in the field concerning heroism. Carter desires to go out and protect the people full-time, although Alice disagrees with such a proposition, as it would place not only Ricky, but Nathan in more harm than they already are.

"I have to ask. Is the government still giving you trouble?" Ricky asked.

"You seriously have to ask me that?" Nathan chuckled. "I thought you would know that."

"I don't know everything."

Nathan nodded.

"No. they've left me be. Last I saw, they were fighting amongst themselves. Funny huh."

A secretary entered the office as they laughed, gaining their focus.

"Excuse me, but, you have a visitor."

"A visitor?' Nathan asked. "What do you mean?"

"You had a scheduled meeting today." Alice replied.

"I did?" Nathan gestured with his hands. "Didn't remember."

The secretary left the office as the visitor entered. Nathan stood up and approached the visitor, shaking his hand.

"Nice to meet you."

"It was in all good time."

"What's your name again?" Nathan asked. "Because I wasn't informed of it clearly."

'Giovanni Marko."

"Ah. Marko. Sounds familiar. You sure you aren't related to some chemist? No scientists in your family?"

"There's one. But, it's not much in the details to discuss."

"Well, that's why we're here. To bring forth what our forefathers could not. Due to the tech of their time."

Nathan and Giovanni sit at the table while Alice and Rick take their leave. Nathan sighed as Giovanni grinned.

"Now, I hear you wanted to present something to me. An idea of sorts."

"Yes. I am aware that you're investing in nanotechnology and I've heard some words across the wind regarding your future venture into hydroelectric technology."

"You have? Huh. Neat."

"But, I believe I might have something that may interest you. Something of value."

"Very well. Nathan replied, leaning in. "I'm all ears."

Giovanni reached into his bag, taking out a diagram. He laid it down on the desk, spreading it out for Nathan to see in full. Nathan's eyes raised as he nodded, seeing the design. He searched and one thing caught his attention to where he stopped and pointed.

"Am I positive that's what that says? I'm not hallucinating, am I?"

"No, Mr. Hawke. What you see is Biotech."

"Huh." Nathan gestured. "I have to ask, why go with biotech when there's many other options available?"

"Because biotech has yet to be fully analyzed by the current scientific community."

"Truly. So, what you're proposing, if I get this right. You want to give us the opportunity of working with biotech to what end?"

"A firm replacement for nanotechnology, of course."

Nathan laughed, yet Giovanni was still.

"I'm not sure I can allow that to happen."

"Give it a test run and afterwards, simply contact me on its operations. Allow a chance."

Nathan looked between Giovanni and the diagram. He nodded slowly and pointed.

"I'll give it a try tonight. See how things work."

"Thank you."

"You might get a reply in the morning. I tend to work very fast."

"As long as you try it out, Mr. Hawke. That's all I wanted to hear."

Giovanni stood up from the desk and the two shook hands before Marko made his leave. Afterwards, Alice returned to the office, seeing Nathan looking at the diagram.

"What is that?"

"This is what Mr. Marko left behind. Said he wants me to test it out."

"And are you?"

"Of course." Nathan smiled. "I'm only doing it to see if what this guy has presented is fact. I'm not replacing nanotech with biotech. It's ridiculous. For the moment. But, I'm not replacing it. I can't."

Late in the night, Nathan sat in the nano-bunker, working on a prototype exosuit with the biotech diagram sitting beside him. He replaced all the nanotech with biotech and upon completing the prototype, the exosuit worked. Yet, it did not match the strength and might of the nano-based suits. Nathan sighed.

"I gave it a try at least. Stuff not's strong enough. Capable. But not equipped."

Elsewhere, Marko worked in his own lab. Standing before him was an armored suit of his own. Similar to the Nano Man armor, yet with more of a dense feature. The eyes appeared bleak as did the whole face. The armor was a dark silver with a black and white glow coming from the area where the veins of a body are located. Marko connected a small battery made completely of biotech into the chest piece and upon the connection, the armor powered up to Marko's pleasure. He grinned looking into the eyes of his own exosuit.

II

BIOTECHNOLOGY

The next day, Nathan and Ricky both were inside the nano-bunker with Nathan measuring out the details pertaining to his and Ricky's exosuits. Ricky looked around at the amount of Nano Man armors which Nathan had built since the appearance of the risen heroes. It was as if Ricky was walking through a large, very large closet for coats. He nodded, taking a gander to the armors, while glancing at Nathan working.

"So, I have to ask, do each of these suits come with something specific to them?"

"Yes. The one you're standing in front of is designed for underwater exploration."

"Ah. And what of this one?" Ricky asked, pointing toward the sleeker one with similar colors to Nano Man's midnight teal and silver design.

"That one is tricky. To an extent."

"What do you mean by tricky?"

"It's an upgraded one to my current. That's all. Told you. Tricky."

"That's not tricky, Nathan. That's just an excuse to hype up the suit."

Nathan chuckled while Ricky continued looking. He stopped in front of one. Larger than the others in size and height. The bulkiness of the suit impressed Ricky. Its presence intrigued Ricky. He was mesmerized by the show of colors with midnight teal layered with gold.

"And what about this one?"

"Which one?" Nathan replied.

"This one right here. The big one."

Nathan looked up from the suit toward him and saw Ricky standing in front of the armor. He stared for a moment and with a serious notion in his eyes, he pointed toward it.

"That's for a contingency."

"Contingency? For what?"

"Not for what. For whom."

"And I take it you have a name for this one?"

"I do. It's called *Beasthunter*."

"I see." Ricky nodded. "Thing looks like a beast."

"Not like the one it's made to combat. Anyhow, want to go ahead and test these things out?"

"I'm up for it."

Nathan and Ricky suited up in their Nano Man and Silver Eagle armors. Flying out of the bunker and into the air on a clear sunny day. Throughout their time in the sky, the two tested the flight strengths of the armors and the speediness of them. Ricky was enjoying the moment, even with a small touch of seriousness in his movement. Nathan just savored the moment. They flew for miles. Even flying through the air above Newark to where the civilians looked up and saw them. Many cheered as they saw Nano Man and Silver Eagle above them.

"They love us." Nathan giggled."

"Alright celebrity-head." Ricky replied. "Keep your focus on the flying."

"I think it's time we return to the bunker, Nathan."

"Yeah, I'm with you. Meet you there."

Nano Man moved with speed in front of Silver Eagle and

without notice, an energy blast impacted Nano Man in the back from behind, causing him to stumble in the air. Silver Eagle turned around and was also attacked by the similar beam. The two caught themselves in the air, turning to see where the attacks had originated from. What they saw was another suit of armor. Only different in appearance to theirs.

"One of yours?" Ricky asked.

"No."

"You're sure?"

"Yeah. I'm sure. We run on nanotech. What I'm reading off that one. It's biotech."

"It's about time we meet." The mysterious armorer spoke.

"And who might you be?" Nano Man asked. "Biotech-1?"

"I am the Bio Man and your age of nanotechnology has come to an end."

"Where did you get that from?" Silver Eagle wondered."

"Calculations and practices."

"Ricky, you're up for a quick fight?"

"I'm right behind you."

Nano Man and Silver Eagle bolted toward the Bio Man, who moved with such speed unlike their own suits. Bio Man slammed his elbow into Silver Eagle's back, crashing him into the ground. He turned without fail, snatching Nano Man by his throat and holding him tightly.

"You think you're the clever one. The one with all the answers. Yet, I know the truth."

"The truth. What truth?"

"That your resource has a limit. Mine does not. I am forever. You are temporary."

Bio Man tossed Nano Man in the air, flying above him and slamming both his feet into Nano Man's chest and coming down into the ground, causing a minor explosion with dirt covering the air. Bio Man looked down, seeing the heroes unconscious on the ground. He let out a chuckle and bolted away.

III

CHOOSE YOUR TECH

Nathan and Ricky returned to Hawke's mansion, bruised up and groggy to Alice's surprise when she saw them coming up the stairs into the home. She rushed over, helping them inside.

"Figured you would be here." Nathan said.

"Where else would I be?"

"Uh, I'm not sure."

From the inside rushed over Brian Neutron, who tossed in his support for them as they entered the mansion.

"We need to go to the bunker." Nathan said.

"Sure thing, boss." Brian replied.

They entered the bunker with Nathan taking his steps on his own and entering the chamber, removing the suit. Ricky followed after and they sat down at the table alongside Alice and Brian. Nathan and Ricky were worn-out, breathing in pain.

"What happened?" Brian asked.

"We were ambushed." Ricky replied.

"By who or what?" Alice wondered. "Nate, what happened?"

"We were attacked by someone wearing a suit of their own. Somewhat like ours, but, powered with biotech instead of nano."

"Another suit-wearer?" Brian said. "How is that possible?"

"Because, the tech is available worldwide. Anyone with the capabilities could manufacture exosuits of their own."

"Well, do you have any clues as to who could've been in the suit?" Alice asked.

"Well, I have one person in mind. Wouldn't be a shocker."

"Who do you mean?" Ricky wondered.

"Earlier I had a meeting with a Mr. Giovanni Marko. He came to me with a proposition in technology. He presented biotech in a way I've seen before, yet, not in such style. He showed me a diagram. I looked at it and didn't mention it to him, but, the diagram was of a suit of armor. Powered by biotech."

"And you're just now telling us this." Ricky replied.

"I wasn't aware he had completed the suit." Nathan sighed. "Anyhow, that explains how he got the jump on us. His suit is powered by some form of enhanced biotech. Plus, he caught us off guard."

"What are you going to do now?" Alice asked with caution. "I mean, you can't just go back out there and find him."

Nathan paused with a nod.

"Why not."

Alice threw up her hands as Brian was concerned for Nathan's well0being. Ricky stayed silent as Nathan chuckled, pointing at the armory of suits behind them.

"I mean. he came to us like a surprise. Why don't we repay him with a surprise of our own."

"You know where he is?" Ricky asked. "I mean, just in case you lead us to some bystander's homestead and we blow up the place. Call it collateral damage afterwards.?"

"I know where he might be. Just not sure.

"Oh, Nate. There's no need to go back out there. Look, why don't you go out first thing in the morning. Your body needs to rest."

"I get that Alice. But, I also know I cannot allow a man like Giovanni to continue roaming free out there. Not after what he did to me and Ricky. So, we'll get ourselves prepped and ready to go back out there, find the guy and give him a beating of his own. Simple."

Ricky stood up with a sigh, holding his hip in pain. He looked toward Nathan and nodded.

"We're good. Alice, trust me. We'll find Giovanni. Finish all of this and we'll be back before midnight strikes."

"Funny. Not funny."

"It wasn't a joke. It was only a reference."

"I get it, Nathan."

Nathan smiled as he glanced over toward his armor. Seeing its damaged and in need of repair. He sighed and focused his sight on the others. He walked over toward them, glancing around them like clothing in a hanger. He stopped in front of one and clapped his hands, startling Alice, Brian, and Ricky. They looked over to him with stern faces. Nathan only showed a grin.

"Oh, I'm sorry. It's just something I do."

"Is that right?" Ricky said.

"Yes. I'm often in here alone. This is my cave, by the way. If Swordman and Taltus can have lairs, I can have one of my own."

"Touché."

Nathan opened one of the armor pods, moving aside as the suit slid out. Ricky saw Nathan prepping the armor and chuckled. Nathan looked over to him with a confused gesture. Rubbing his beard with question.

"What's so funny?"

"Nothing. Figured that suit would be your next pick."

"Like I said, it's an upgraded model. Perfect time to try it out."

"I'm sure. I'm ready when you are."

IV

<u>WAYS TO END A WAR</u>

Nano Man and silver Eagle flew high above Newark across the night sky. They moved forward toward the trees in the distance.

"Where are we headed, Nate?"

"To the park."

"Why the park? Why not the city streets?"

"Because there's no need to have innocent civilians caught up in the crossfire. You know how this stuff works."

"But does Giovanni?"

"I guess we'll find out."

The two flew out into the trees and Nano Man landed. Silver Eagle glanced around the area, seeing nothing. Tossing his hands up with confusion as he turned his focus back toward Nathan.

"Why are we out here?"

"Trust me. He's coming."

Above them came down Giovanni, his suit surging with energy. Nano Man raised his hands as did Eagle. Giovanni applauded their reflex of skill.

"I had a sense you would be out here." Giovanni said. "Funny."

"That's not funny." Nano Man replied. "That's just a saying."

"Well, like all good things. They begin and they end."

"You're talking about us or something else?" Eagle asked.

"You'll see."

Giovanni hovered with great speed, blasting toward them with biotech energy beams. Nano Man and Silver Eagle bolted from the ongoing attacks. They circled Bio Man as he turned firing the energy. It was as it would not stop.

"We need to do something." Eagle said.

"Strike low." Nano Man replied. "I'll strike high."

"You're sure about this?"

"Only way to find out is to do it."

The two combined slam Bio Man into the ground, burrowing him deep into the dirt. Nano Man and Silver Eagle fly out of the hole and land nearby. They walked toward the hole, seeing only the searing smoke from Giovanni's armor. Nano Man jumped in, taking Giovanni out of the armor as it exploded.

"My work." Giovanni uttered.

"Told you. Biotech isn't all that."

Giovanni was later taken to a secure facility. While inside, he was greeted by a visitor who caught him off guard. Giovanni stood to attention with his hand extended.

"About time we meet." The visitor said.

"It's a pleasure, Mr. Cramer."

"Now, you know why I'm here."

"The armor is gone. Nano Man and his friend destroyed it."

"That right?"

"Why else am I in here."

"A guy like you doesn't just design one suit of armor. You design several. Plenty more to go around."

"So, the plan is still in effect?"

"Of course. I've already gotten Peters taken care of. Niles will cover your troubles. Meanwhile, I have a few others to gather before we make our move."

"Once the plan is in effect, what of Nathan and his allies?"

"Leave them to me and Niles."

I

THE POURING OF BLOOD

Commander Norland and his team of Champions received Intel regarding an ADDER base set up in Siberia. Norland prepped the team on the details as they headed out. While in the hoverjet, Norland and the Champions were given more information concerning the base's whereabouts within Siberia by T.I.T.A.N. Agent Mariah Cooper.

"This won't be like last time, right?" Fields asked with a smile.

"No. We don't think there are any snowman in this region." Cooper replied. "That we know of."

"I see."

Norland sat next to Steve Nixon as the others chatted with each other. General Sarge Hunter was also onboard the hoverjet, to which Norland was supposed to see him accompany. Even Nixon was a little thrown off by Hunter's presence on the field.

"Why'd he come?" Nixon wondered.

"Probably to keep tabs on a few of us. Preferably Woods or Carl."

"What of Andrea?"

"Maybe." Norland replied. "Not sure. Although, you can ask. I'm sure he'll give you an answer."

"Not going to."

Norland laughed as they arrived at the location in Siberia.

Deep within the mountains, covered in snow. The team was prepared for the wintry environment. They lowered the hoverjet for the team to rope themselves out. Norland was last to exit the jet as he led the team through the grounds.

"How far along is this base of theirs?" Nixon asked.

"Not far." Hunter replied. "What's wrong? Too cold for you?"

"No sir. Just curious is all."

While they walked for a certain set of miles, Norland looked ahead of them, seeing a structure. To his eyes, it was a wall made of brick. He pointed toward it, gathering the attention of the team.

"This must be the place."

"Hmm." Hunter said. "Your eyes prove well."

"Ok." Carl said. "So, how do we find a way inside?"

Andrea looked down, smearing the snow beneath her feet to the side, revealing themselves standing atop a window. She stepped back, stomping. Norland approached her, looking down at the window. He nodded.

"Keep going." Norland said.

Andrea stomped several times as the glass cracked. Norland could tell the glass was dense due to the amount of ice. Norland smashed his feet into the ice, breaking through the window as the others stepped back. Andrea used her whips to rope into the base as the others followed. The height of the base was about two stories tall. They looked around at the interior. Seeing frozen wooden chairs and metal desks. File cabinets were tightly closed due to the temperatures. Sarge pulled out his flashlight, looking at the interior. Only hearing the slight chills of the cold winds.

"Yep. This is the place."

"You know it already?" Nixon asked.

"Yeah. Because who else would put a base out here in a place like this."

"We're near Russia, aren't we?" Woody said.

"Figures." Hunter replied.

Norland stepped forward, seeing a hallway ahead of them. "Let's check down here."

The team followed Norland down the hall as they were led to an open area. In front of them were two paths of steps leading to the second floor where a double door was centered.

"We go up there and find what may have been left behind."

"Left behind?" A voice echoed from the second floor.

They raised their weapons, Norland's fists covered themselves in ice as they looked up at the doors opening, hearing the echoing footsteps inching closer. On the balcony, they saw a man cloaked in a dirty hood. His face shrouded.

"The hell are you supposed to be?" Sarge asked. "The grim reaper?"

"Not exactly. Although, we share much in common."

"Why are you out here?" Norland asked.

"I can say the same about the rest of you. You all seek something which does not belong to you. You invade a foreign base without any invitation."

"We don't need no invitation when it comes to those aligned with ADDER." Sarge referenced. "Such like yourself."

"ADDER. I only do a handful of work for them. But, I am not one of them."

"Then, why are you here?" Norland asked again. "Tell us something."

"Count Blood."

"Count Blood?" Sarge said. "The hell's that mean?"

"That's my name. Count Blood."

"Well then, Count Blood," Norland replied. "Why are you here. Out in the mountains of ice, alone?"

"Who said I was alone?"

Rushing behind Blood were a dozen ADDER agents, all armed and armored. The Champions circled themselves around

Norland and Hunter. Sarge cocked his gun, aimed toward Blood.

"You send your guys toward us, I'll blow a hole through that skull of yours."

"I'll see if you can." Blood raised his arms as the ADDER agents jumped down from the balcony, colliding with Norland and the Champions. Sarge fired several rounds at the agents rushing toward him, making his way up the stairs. Norland jabbed and kicked the agents as he helped his team. Sarge made it to the second floor and Blood had vanished. The doors were open, only revealing a hallway of office space. Norland and the Champions took down the agents and followed Hunter upstairs.

"What have you found, Sarge?" Norland asked.

"Nothing. This place was only a decoy."

"They knew we were coming."

II

<u>PEP TALK</u>

The team returned to the T.I.T.A.N. headquarters, meeting with Colonel Evan Nader and Sonya Rowlings in the main office. They gave the details regarding the ADDER base, revealing the details of Count Blood and their fight against the ADDER agents who were with him. Nader nodded and stood up, looking out through the window.

"We've known about Blood for some time now."

"You're serious?" Sarge asked.

"Yes, General Hunter. Although, we only though of him to be some kind of small fry. A foe for someone like the risen heroes to take down. We didn't expect him to be aligned with ADDER. By any reason."

"Count Blood is not the boss of ADDER right now." Sonya added. "We discovered more detail when we tracked Blood's previous actions across northern Asia."

"And what did you find?" Norland questioned.

"Blood is working for someone else."

"Who is this 'someone else'?" Norland asked. "Is it Kozlov? Madame Cobra?"

"None of the above, Commander." Nader replied. "The only name we've been able to track down concerning Blood's boss is peculiar. He goes by the name of the Royal Ghost."

"Royal Ghost?" Norland said. "Never heard of him before."

"Because that's part of his play." Nader replied. "The Royal Ghost was always thought to be some sort of practical codename in order for ADDER agents to sneak into places that aren't theirs. An internal means of espionage."

"So, Blood is working for Ghost. But, Ghost has to be working for someone as well. Or with someone."

"That's where we're currently placed." Nader said. "Right now, we'll do our best to track down any leads that may direct us to Blood or Ghost or whomever is helping them in this cause of theirs."

"Keep me updated." Norland said.

"Will do." Sonya replied with a smile.

Norland nodded and left the office and walked down the hallway toward Professor Flm's laboratory. He entered, seeing Flm's scientific methods being put to use as they always are. Flm sat at his desk, looking over some files as Norland approached him. Flm looked up, seeing the Commander.

"Wasn't expecting you today."

"When do you expect me?" Norland laughed. "I just wanted to see how you were after all that's transpired over these past few months."

"I'm doing well with all that's considered. I heard the news of your little event in Siberia. What have you been able to find so far?"

"From what Nader and Rowlings have said, this Count Blood figure works for someone called the Royal Ghost."

Flm rubbed his chin, nodding.

"Royal Ghost." Film said. "Sounds like a codename to me."

"So I've been told."

"What are you going to do about it?"

"Well, once they come up with some new Intel, me and the Champions will head out and see what we can do."

"And just you and your team?"

"Yeah. Why?"

"Couldn't you contact the others?"

"Others?"

"You're other compatriots."

Norland grinned. Shaking his head with a slight nod.

"I believe they're busy with their own affairs."

"Eh. Well, that's a possibility." Flm replied. "But, never say never to the cause."

"I'll keep that in mind."

Elsewhere, Count Blood entered a secure room. In front of him was only a large table with five seats. Standing in the room as Blood walked toward the table were ADDER agents, armed and loaded.

"Where are the others?" Blood questioned.

"They're on their way." An Agent responded.

"Very well." Blood said, sitting down at the table.

Across from him were several other doors into the room. He looked toward the one on his left as it opened, seeing the Iron Crane entering alongside Madame Cobra. Blood nodded, standing up and extending his hand toward Crane.

"A pleasure we meet."

"Likewise." Crane said. "I take it you must be this Count Blood I've heard about."

"That I am. Nice to meet you, Madame."

"Enough with the flattering. Where's the others?"

"They're on their way, ma'am." The agent replied.

The door on the right of Blood opened, entering a man dressed in all black, wearing a black leather trench coat. He presented himself with a stern countenance. Nodding toward the others.

"It's an honor to meet others with like minds." The man said.

"You're this doctor, right?" Cobra asked.

"A doctor amongst many things. Please, call me Nicholas

Jovano."

Jovano sat at the table, looking at the agents. He nodded with a keen grin.

"This all he brought?" Jovano asked, pointing at the agents. "I thought there would be more."

"The others were sent to another location." Crane said. "To keep watch."

"To keep watch for whom?"

"T.I.T.A.N. and their heroes." Blood said. "I ran into them in Siberia at the old facility."

"So, they're aware of us?" Jovano added. "Well, the three of you. I wouldn't worry."

"How come?" Cobra questioned.

"Because this Commander of theirs hasn't met me."

"You said you were a doctor?" Crane referenced. "What can a doctor do against a soldier with abilities beyond natural comprehension?"

"As I said, I am a doctor amongst many things."

From the door facing Blood, entered the Royal Ghost himself alongside two large ADDER agents. Wearing armor on their arms, chest, and legs. Their helmets resembled the helmets worn by ancient Romans. The Royal Ghost removed his golden crown and red cloaked hood as he sat at the table.

"Good of us all to meet this day. Now, let's begin with the plan."

"T.I.T.A.N. found the Siberian base." Blood said. "I and my men did what we could."

"You did what was needed. I am sure they're searching for us at this very moment and want them to find us."

"Find us?!" Crane said. "For what cause?!"

"Yes." Cobra said. "Please elaborate for us as to what your plan might be?"

Ghost looked over toward Jovano, who sat silent.

"The best way to deal with these heroes and soldiers is to face them head-on."

"Head-on?" Blood asked. "But, we do not have enough agents to combat them."

"We have all we need."

"And that is?" Cobra asked, looking at everyone in the room.

"These agents. Us and Jovano."

"I must know," Crane said. "who is this guy and why is he here?"

"Nicholas Jovano is a man of many talents and he will be the best case against these T.I.T.A.N. fools. Their Commander Norland in particular."

"While you all deal with T.I.T.A.N., I will handle their Commander."

"And what gives you that right?" Crane wondered. "Why are you in this position to begin with?"

"Well, Mr. Kozlov. I'm a doctor and a businessman. This is all business."

Ghost turned around toward one of the armored agents, handing him a device. The agent took the device and left the room. Crane stared with confusion.

"What did you give him?" Cobra asked.

"Well, a way for T.I.T.A.N. to find us."

"You mean a tracking device?" Crane yelled.

"Of course. We need them to know we're here."

"What is your game, Ghost?"

"This is not a game. Just as Mr. Jovano said, it's business."

"The hell's your problem." Crane said. "This is not how ADDER operates."

"It's how they operate now." Ghost stated. "I suggest you prepare yourselves for the coming fight."

"I am ready." Jovano said.

III

THE STRANGER AND THE BROTHER

Within the T.I.T.A.N. headquarters, Agent Cooper entered the office where Nader, Hunter, and Norland were speaking with haste. She presented them with a device, showing a signal mark related to ADDER.

"Where is this location?" Nader asked.

"In the arctic."

"Didn't we just leave that place?" Hunter said.

"No." Norland replied. "I think she means north from Siberia. Much north."

"So, when are we heading out?" Hunter said.

"I'll get the team ready." Cooper said, leaving the office.

The team gathered together, equipped and ready. Norland looked ahead, seeing Nader entering the hoverjet. Unsure, he approached him as he entered himself.

"You're coming as well?" Norland asked.

"Figure I should get out in the field every once and a while." Norland nodded.

"Cool." Norland replied, sitting down.

Entering the jet behind Norland were the Champions, Agent Mara, Lady Siren, and General Hunter. They took off, heading for the arctic. On their way there, Norland talked with Nader concerning the possibilities of an ambush. Nader was intrigued by

Norland's thoughts.

"What will we do if there's an ambush like you believe?" Nader asked.

"Simple. We take them head-on. If ADDER truly is operating in that base, we need to stop them. By any cost."

Nader sat back in his seat, nodding his head.

"I guess we'll see how this goes."

"Only chance we have."

Norland and his team made their arrival into the arctic and within the horizon, Norland spotted several helicopters ahead. He pointed, knowing it was the ADDER base.

"They didn't bother to keep themselves hidden." Nader noticed.

"You think they want us to know?" Hunter asked.

"Possibly." Norland replied. "Either way, we're here."

The team gathered their gear as they landed near the base. From there, the team split into pairs. Norland with Nader, Rowlings, and Nixon. Whiplash with Hunter, Hawk, and Eagle. Mariah and Jessica remained with the hoverjet. Once they made their way toward the doors, ADDER agents quickly spawned, firing toward them. Nader and Hunter took them out quickly with several rounds.

"They know we're here." Hunter said.

"That was the plan." Norland replied. "Alright, everyone knows their place. Now, let's get this done. Find Count Blood and this Royal Ghost."

Inside the ADDER base, which was as blue as the morning sky, coated in ice and sunlight, yet with banners of ADDER across the walls and doorways, they saw three paths in front of them. Unsure of which direction, Norland, Rowlings, and Nixon both went on the left while Nader and Hunter took the center path, leaving the right path for Whiplash, Hawk, and Eagle. Down the right path, the three Champions were confronted by more ADDER agents, this time, armored with greater firearms. Whiplash extended her arm-whips, slashing against the agents' armor while Hawk and Eagle dodged he surrounding fire with their shields.

Down the center path, Nader and Hunter both shoot toward the agents in their sights. From the first and second floors. The whole event was reminiscent of their days during the Republic War, yet only this time battling against an organization. Nader looked ahead on he second floor, seeing three more agents running in. He pointed as Hunter fired his shots with his glock. Nader reached to his side, raising up another glock, double-wielding glocks.

"Wonder how the others are doing." Hunter yelled.

"I'm sure they got it covered."

Within the path of the left side, Norland, Rowlings, and Nixon were confronted by no one. Surprising them, they discovered themselves entering a laboratory. Filled with tables, computers, and a large screen resting on the wall. within the room, Norland looked and saw someone sitting down at the desk. Nixon raised his gun, firing a shot against the wall. The one who was sitting at the desk raised his head and stood up, yet, not turned toward them. Norland stepped forward.

"Who are you?"

The man didn't turn to face them. Nixon fired another shot, now the man only laughed.

"He asked who are you." Rowlings said. "Tell us now or you'll regret it later."

"Regret what?" The man said. "Your defeat?"

The man turned toward them, revealing himself to them.

"I was waiting for you to arrive, Commander Norland."

"You know who I am."

"Yes, and why you're here."

"And you must be?" Nixon asked.

"Jovano. Nicholas Jovano."

"Well, Mr. Jovano, you're going to tell us where's Count Blood and Royal Ghost."

"I'm not going to tell you anything other than what must be done."

"And what will be done?" Rowlings asked.

"Your defeat."

"I've heard enough." Nixon said, raising his gun and firing another shot.

The bullet rushed toward Jovano and within a nanosecond, Jovano caught the round, holding it between his fingers. He grinned as he dropped it.

"What are you?" Norland asked.

"I'm the evolution of humanity. I am the future."

"We have to take him out." Nixon said.

"Your move, Commander." Rowlings said.

Norland sighed.

"On me!"

They went and attacked Jovano, only their attacks weren't making any impacts. Jovano dodged their movements in such speed, he appeared invisible to their sights. Jovano stopped, grabbing Nixon by the throat and slamming him on a desk. He rushed toward Siren, elbowing her in the abdomen and tossing her against the wall. Norland paused himself, turning around toward Jovano.

"How are you doing this?" Norland wondered.

"I have my ways."

"I wasn't aware I would be fighting a ghost." Nixon said.

"I'm not dead. Just evolved."

Nixon fired more rounds toward Jovano. He continued dodging and grabbing the bullets before throwing one of them into Nixon's chest at great speed. Rowlings latched onto Jovano's back, punching him in the chest. Jovano grunting, snatched her by the hair and slammed her into the floor. Norland rushed into the fight with Jovano, matching him in strength. Norland punched Jovano in the face and kneed him in the chest before Jovano could grab him by the throat, holding him off his feet and throwing him into the large screen.

"This was easier than I anticipated." Jovano sighed. "Perhaps, we can do this another time, Commander Norland."

Jovano walked toward another door on the other end of the lab, revealing them to have been on the second floor of the base, standing over a large canyon. Nixon stood up and ran toward Jovano. Norland yelled for him to stop, yet he ignored the command, spearing Jovano through the door and onto the ledge on the outside. Norland stood up to reach the door as Jovano pummeled Nixon in such speed before holding him by the neck and tossing him off the ledge. Nixon fell into the canyon just as Norland tackled Jovano off the ledge, yet he glided himself to the icy grounds with his trench coat. Norland and Rowlings looked down into the canyon, unable to find Nixon. Norland shook his head with tears flowing from his eyes.

"Commander." Rowlings said. "We need to find the others."

Norland nodded, still looking into the canyon. Rowlings placed her hand on Norland's own.

"Adam. Come on."

IV

FALLEN COMRADES

Nader and Hunter continued firing at the ADDER agents as Norland and Rowlings, entered shooting at the remaining agents. Most of them fled once they saw Norland. Nader glanced toward them and stopped with a stare.

"Where's Nixon?"

"He didn't make it." Norland said.

"The hell!" Hunter yelled.

"What do you mean by he didn't make it?"

"We ran into this scientist guy." Rowling replied. "He was stronger than we thought."

"What happened to Nixon?" Nader asked.

"The scientist tossed him off the ledge into the canyon." Norland said. "I couldn't get to him in time."

"And what of this 'scientist'?"

"He escaped." Rowlings answered. "Glided from the ledge to the ground outside."

Nader sighed heavily. Shaking his head.

"What of the Royal Ghost?" Norland asked.

"We haven't seen him." Hunter said. "We should find the others. See if they've confronted the guy."

They walked out to the entry point of the paths just as Whiplash, Hawk, and Eagle were doing the same. They all stared at each other. No sign of the Royal Ghost. Not even Count Blood, Iron Crane, or Madame Cobra. Norland shook his head and walked outside. Reaching the canyon ledge. He looked down, only seeing ice and water. Rowlings stood besides him.

"Maybe he fell into the water." Norland said.

"We don't know that."

"But, there's still a chance. There has to be."

"I know he's your comrade, Adam. But, you saw how that scientist threw him. Nixon couldn't survive that fall even with water below."

"There's always a chance. A possibility."

"I know. I know." Rowlings sighed. "I'll speak with some of the others. Send some agents down there to check. See what they find."

"Thanks." Norland nodded.

After several hours of searching, the T.I.T.A.N. agents were unable to find Nixon's body. Norland took the news with much grief, yet it did not change his countenance by any means. He boarded the hoverjet with the others and returned to the headquarters. Back at the headquarters, a memorial was set for Steve Nixon, a fellow comrade and loyal soldier to the cause.

Outside the headquarters, Norland stood alone and coming toward him in the air was Taltus. Norland and the titagod shook hands. Taltus heard of Nixon's death and stood beside Norland during the memorial.

"You look like you have something to say." Norland said.

"I've already told Kenari. Now, I'm telling you. There's something coming."

"Something? Such as?"

"A dire force from another realm."

"Similar to the Retropolis event?"

"Worse."
Norland sighed.
"When do we start the mission?"

THE UNSTOPPABLE BEAST: THE HIDDEN JUNGLE

I

THE MYTH OF THE JAGUAR

The U.S. Military roll into the Amazon Rainforest with over a dozen jeeps. Rain poured down heavily over them, causing the ground to become murky. Mud flung across the grounds from the roaming jeeps. The jeeps drove into the forest, stopping at a particular point. Afterwards, tents were set up as the area was developed into a base of operations. Sitting in one was General Lawler, gazing over a map of the forest. Lawler sighed.

"This is the place. I'm certain of it."

Lawler exited the jeep, entering the larger tent, where he saw other soldiers, some with laptops, metal detectors, and maps. Lawler sat down at the main desk, laying the map of the rainforest down. Another soldier approached the desk.

"What is it?" Lawler asked.

"We've found it."

Lawler's face froze. Standing up from his seat and following the soldier back to the outside. There, Lawler caught glimpse of two soldiers carrying a large object. Smothered in dirt. They placed the object in a container. Lawler stood over it, wiping his hand over it, revealing a glyph of a jaguar.

"Is this is, sir?" A soldier asked.

"Yes, soldier. This is what we're after. Bring it inside. We'll clean it up and study it further."

The soldiers carried the object into the tent. Lawler let out a grin, nodding his head as he entered the tent. Returning inside, Lawler looked down at the object. Standing by was another soldier, keen on the object. Lawler noticed him.

"What is it?"

"Since that is what we've been searching for, does that prove the creature's existence?"

"The Jaguar, you mean."

"Yes sir. Does it prove it's real? Is it out here among us?"

"Soldier, once we study this thing, we'll know for sure. But for right now, as long as we have this, we have the Jaguar in our control."

In another place within the Amazon, Kent Brock arrived. Exiting a jeep himself. Raising up his binoculars, looking out in the distance, seeing the military's camp.

"They've already found it."

II
THE RUSTLING IN THE TREES

Several hours had passed, giving Kent the opportunity to sneak closer to the military camp. He looked ahead while hiding in the bushes, seeing the soldiers walking into their tents while Lawler remained inside the larger one. Kent went ahead as the soldiers were sleep. Lawler, however was not as he exited the large tent, walking toward a smaller one nearby. He went inside and closed it up. Kent nodded, making his move to the large tent.

Once inside, he went straight for Lawler's desk and what he discovered were files. Many of them sealed in folders. He opened one, reading the pages. They were confidential documents. He continued on before coming across a page which detailed their true intent in the Amazon. Describing the object which Lawler had earlier. Kent turned to his left, seeing the object on a shelf nearby.

"The myth is real?" Kent uttered to himself.

He snatched as many files as possible and dove out of the tent, bumping into three soldiers. They paused hesitating, seeing Kent. He stared before continuing his run. The soldiers yelled, rallying the others out of their sleep to apprehend Kent. Lawler arose and bolted from his tent, he looked out, seeing Kent with the folders.

"Son of a bitch."

Kent ran into the trees as the soldiers chased him, some began firing their weapons into the bushes, hoping to hit Kent. Lawler ran into the large tent and toward his desk, seeing several folders were missing. He shook his head in anger and let out a loud scream. Lawler grabbed the tablet, he stared silent. A grin grew upon his face.

"Since we're having such a difficult time finding him, let's see what this thing can do."

Lawler held up the tablet and slammed it to the ground. From the impact emerged dark green mist, covering the grounds of the military's entire camp. The mist caught the attention of the other soldiers and Kent himself. The smoke was near above the tree line as Kent continued running while the three soldiers who stumbled upon him continued their chase. Lawler walked out of the tent, only seeing the smoke which had filled the camp in a thick blanket of smoke. From that moment, Lawler slowly returned to his tent and sealed it up while the soldiers gazed around the camp, their firearms in hand as a loud roar emerged from the trees near them. Kent paused in his steps, hearing the roar.

"Oh no."

The soldiers at the camp instantly started firing their weapons toward the trees within the thick smoke. A rushing sound echoed around them from the trees as the sound of moving leaves quickened their steps. The cracking of branches instilled fear into their minds as they continued shooting. They paused, hearing nothing. Within a second, a large figure lunged from the trees into the thick smoke toward the soldiers, slashing their throats and mauling them. The other soldiers saw the figure, shooting it, yet its hide was too dense for the bullets to penetrate.

Kent continued running and paused himself for a quick breather. Putting the folders into his bag. The three soldiers walked silently through the forest searching for him.

"We should return to camp." One soldier said.

"No. Not until we find Brock. He's the reason why we're out here in the first place."

"You don't hear that shooting?" The third soldier asked. "Something's happening back at camp. We have to return to help the others."

Kent exhaled and took off running again. The soldiers caught him. The first one raised his rifle and fired a shot, impacting Kent in the left calf. Kent yelled in pain as he fell to the ground. Kent tossed his bag over to the nearby tree as he clutched his leg. The three soldiers approached him, staring him down.

"You thought you were getting away from us, Brock."

"You don't know what you've done." Kent replied. "Best you run."

"Or what?"

"Go help your fellow comrades, soldier." Kent said slowly. "Before he comes out."

"Before who comes out?"

"He's crawling his way to the top." Kent said. "Run! Get out of here now!"

The third soldier started to think. He looked down at Kent and toward his leg. The details flowing in. he stepped back without hesitation.

"We need to go now."

"What's got you spooked." The first soldier asked. "He's just a man."

"You don't know, do you?"

"Know what?"

"Kent Brock. The reason why Lawler is after him."

"He's a fugitive. Nothing more."

"He is more and it's coming out."

The first soldier glanced down at Kent, who began to shiver as his body twisted. The third soldier ran off with the second one to follow. The first yelled for them to return. His back turned from

Kent, who's body began transforming. Growing in size. Once the soldier turned back to Brock, he wasn't looking at Kent. He raised his head up slowly, seeing the dark red glowing eyes of the Beast. The Beast roared, snatching the soldier and throwing him into the trees of the forest before letting out another louder roar, gaining attention of what attacked the soldiers as the smoke withered away, revealing the soldiers were attacked and slaughtered by the hidden creature, the Amazon Jaguar.

III

A WORLD OF MONSTERS

The two soldiers made their retreat from the Beast, running back to the camp. In doing so, they found themselves surrounded by their comrades, all dead on the ground, covered in blood and deep claw wounds.

"What happened?"

"They were shooting at something. The question is where did it go?"

They looked around at the tents, seeing nor hearing anyone. Unbeknownst to them, Lawler remained inside his tent, quiet and watching. While the soldiers searched the tents, the Amazon Jaguar lunged from the trees above them to the ground, standing over them in its immense height and size. The soldiers turned around to see the creature and quickly began shooting the creature. Not realizing its hide was too dense for the rounds, the Jaguar snatched one by his threat, ripping his head from his shoulders. It went for the remaining one and after one step, the Beast entered their sights from the opposite angle. The Jaguar turned, glaring toward the Beast, who roared. The soldier made a run for it into the forest as the two monsters shared a stare down.

"Let's see what this creature's made of." Lawler whispered to himself, watching the monsters.

The Jaguar moved with such speed, it caught the Beast off guard and at that moment, the Jaguar swiped its claws into the

Beast's chest, scratching him and seeing the blood. The Beast huffed and speared the Jaguar into the nearby tree, pummeling the creature with a series of blows to the head. The number of punches crack the tree and it falls onto the nearby tents. Lawler continued watching. His focus was steady and set on the fight. The Jaguar arose from underneath the tree, grabbing the Beast by his throat and slamming him to the ground, making its way to gnaw the Beast, yet the Beast was strong enough to hold back the creature's head and sharp fangs.

Sounds of vehicles echoed close by, getting the attention of the two monsters and even Lawler.

"The hell's that?" Lawler said, peaking through the tent.

What he saw were more soldiers and jeeps, this time they came out fully armed. They ran into the camp, seeing the dead soldiers and the two monsters colliding. They began firing their weapons toward them. The Jaguar turned around, gazing with its piercing golden eyes, proceeded to lung toward them with slashes as the Beast arose, jumping atop the Jaguar and slamming the creature into the trees. As the soldiers continued shooting at the Beast and the Jaguar, arrows flew through the air around them, unsure of their origin, the soldiers moved, ducking down and hiding behind the trees. On the opposite end of the camp emerged several tribesmen from the forest, bows and arrows in hand. Their focus was on the soldiers, not the Beast nor the Jaguar.

"Impossible." Lawler said, bolting out of tent, standing between the soldiers and the tribesmen. "Don't shoot them!"

"General." A soldier gestured. "We didn't know you were still alive."

"I kept myself steady. Such as the rest of you shall do."

The Beast and the Jaguar continue their brawl with punches, slashes and kicks. The Beast snatched the Jaguar by his neck, raising him up and slamming him with a choke slam. The Beast stood still, turning his sights toward Lawler and the soldiers. He let out a raging roar as his eyes sparked red. The soldiers ran, except for Lawler, who nodded.

"Next time, Brock."

Lawler made his escape with the remaining soldiers in their jeeps. The beast turned around, seeing the tribesmen. However, the Jaguar was gone. Nowhere to be seen. Confusing the Beast as the tribesmen nodded toward him before disappearing into the forest. The Beast looked around, seeing himself standing in the ruins of the military camp with the deceased soldiers. The Beast roared before leaping into the air and vanishing through the rainforest.

Elsewhere, the tribesmen returned to their homestead, where they began giving thanks and worship toward a large Jaguar statue, with the Jaguar creature itself, crouched in the trees, overseeing their actions with ease.

I

THE WORK OF TWO TEAMS

On the morning, Kenari Clark heard a strange commotion coming from the front yard of the Clark Estate. Moving with haste, Kenari looked out and saw a towering figure standing in the yard, facing the home. The being wielded a large axe and was dressed in the garb of a medieval executioner. Allison glared out the window, seeing the brutish figure.

"I'll give you a hand."

"No. you wait here for now. I'll contact the others. They'll arrive much quicker than expected."

Kenari went down into the Swordlair, quickly opening up the closet of the swordsuit. Also in the closet was a small device. Kenari pressed the button, after sounded a continuous beep. He dressed into the swordsuit, grabbing the sword before he walked outside to confront the figure. Once Swordman had stepped out, facing the tall being, who did not make a move.

"I see the sword-wielder." The figure said.

"You're looking at him." Swordman replied. "Tell me your name and motive?"

"I am the Executioner of the Shadows. I have been summoned here to eliminate the sword-wielder."

"Who summoned you here to kill me?"

"I will not speak their name. Only the death of the sword-wielder."

"What are you waiting for?"

The Executioner raised the axe, slamming into the ground after Swordman jumped out of its way. Swordman moved behind the Executioner, striking the tall figure's legs with his sword, slashing away as dark-colored blood poured from the cuts. The Executioner stumbled. Swordman continued striking until the Executioner grabbed him by his head, tossing him across the field. Swordman stood up, sword clenched in his right hand and as he rushed toward the figure, a sonic boom echoed in the air. Swordman stopped, gazing up as did the Executioner. Above them were Taltus, Nano Man, and Theus. Making their landing next to Swordman. A rushing engine roared from the Estate gates. Over by the front gate A T.I.T.A.N. jeep arrived Norland. Swordman nodded.

"Faster than I expected."

"What's happening in your front

"Who is this thing?" Taltus asked.

"Calls itself the Executioner of the Shadows."

"Executioner of Shadows?" Theus uttered. "I've never heard of such a being in Eragardia."

Nano Man gazed closer toward the Executioner with his nanotech signaling a disturbance in their presence.

"Something else is here."

"Such as?" Taltus asked.

"Magic." Swordman replied.

"Wait?" Nano Man gestured with confusion in his voice. "How did you know?"

"Because there's a portal opening above us."

Looking up at the mysterious violet-shaded portal, from it arrived Kular The Aqua-Barbarian, The Voltage, and Doctor Fortune. They stood beside the Resistance, all facing the Executioner.

"I didn't call you." Swordman said to Fortune.

"No need. I sensed the Executioner's energy."

"Then do whatever you're going to do." Nano Man said.

Fortune raised his hand, taking control of the portal above them. The Executioner glared up toward it, attempting to strike it with the axe, Fortune slammed the portal onto the Executioner, removing him from the land and Fortune closed the portal. Nano Man gently nodded.

"Well, I guess that's over."

"Not quite." Swordman said. "How did you know it was here? Such spirits cannot easily trespass on this land."

"Because there's a more powerful play at work." Fortune replied. "Anyhow, I suggest we try and figure out what brought the Shadow Executioner here onto your land."

II

SKILL OR MAGIC?

The Resistance and The Protectors entered Clark's home. They gazed around, especially Nathan as his Nano Man helmet opened to reveal his face.

"When did you change this around?"

"Sometime ago." Swordman said. "Why do you ask?"

"Sight-seeing is all."

"Where's Kent Brock?" Fortune asked.

"He should be here any minute." Swordman replied. "I sent out a signal to him as well."

"The same one you sent to us?"

"With a minor altercation."

From the front gate arrived Brock, exiting out of a taxicab. He looked out at the size of Kenari's estate as he walked toward the front door. He entered the home and was quickly taken back by the size and detail of the interior.

"Good you've come." Swordman said.

"I see that everyone is dressed for the occasion." Kent said, seeing them in their gear. "Sorry I wasn't able to come fully prepared."

"No need for it right now." Fortune said. "I'm trying to explain to them how the Shadow Executioner could've stepped foot on his land."

"As I said, it's not possible."

"How come?"

"Magic has no place on this land. I've made sure of it."

"Then how am I still here? What did you place on this land? A protection of some kind."

"A prayer to bind any of those who wield magic to suffer a greater threat than losing their power."

"Are you sure your religious ideologies didn't give a way to dark forces to invade?"

"It's never happened until now. Something's taking place and I need to know why."

"Understood. And will I lose my sorcerer skills if I stay here any longer?"

"If you did, you would've lost them as soon as you came out of the portal. This proves someone has been meddling around my territory unseen and I cannot take the option of it being a human."

"You think it might be Death?" Nathan suggested. "I mean, she did have some kind of magic skill on her. I remember feeling it in our last encounter."

"No. this is not her doing. It's someone else."

"Perhaps, if you would allow me to walk throughout your land, I could find a possible source."

Swordman stepped forward toward Fortune.

"Even though I do not trust sorcerers, I will allow you to do so."

"No problem."

Fortune went out and searched all of Kenari's land. From the estate to the farmlands and the vineyards. Upon his return, Fortune concluded there was no magical elements within his land. Swordman nodded. Yet, he is still confused as to how a magical entity could've stepped foot on his land. He glanced at Fortune, thinking to himself.

"This makes you wonder how come I'm still here with my

magic.”

“I was asking myself the same question.”

“Before you jump to conclusions, I did not have anything to do with this.”

“Yet, you quickly rid us of the Executioner. How?”

“I am the Supreme Enchanter after all.”

“And if you weren’t?” Swordman questioned.

“Then, we’ll be fighting the Executioner in your front yard. However, that is not the case. Is it?”

Swordman nodded. Taking some steps back from Fortune, glancing at the other heroes.

“Now what do we do?” Nathan asked. “I mean, where did you send the big guy anyway?”

“In a dimension far from here. There’s no need in worrying about his return.”

“This is not done.” Swordman said. “I need to know how it came about. How you’re standing in my home. Unharmed.”

“Maybe whatever you had placed didn’t exactly work out for you.”

“I have other means of protection, sorcerer.”

“Then, why don’t you use those and get this done with.”

The Swordman pulled out his sword, holding it toward Fortune. The heroes’ steadied themselves. Fortune stood calm, with a hint of a grin on his face.

“Put the sword down.”

“Or what?”

“This doesn’t have to end in a fight.”

“A fight? With you?” Swordman gestured. “It wouldn’t be a fight. Only a slaughter.”

“You honestly believe your little sword can take my magic?”

“This sword taken down those far more powerful than yourself. Don’t push this any further.”

“But, aren’t I pushing it by me just standing here. On your

land. A sorcerer in your presence. In your home."

The Voltage stepped in between the two. Holding his arms out.

"Fortune, there's no need in pushing him."

"Why not?"

"Because he's The Swordman for starters."

"So what? Fortune gestured. "Can The Swordman defeat the Supreme Enchanter?"

"What are you doing, Doctor?" Nathan asked.

"I'm doing what I've wanted to for a while now. This man needs some manners in the arts of spiritual warfare."

"Manners in spiritual warfare? You have no idea the meaning of the war."

"Try me."

Kent stepped back into a corner as Voltage and Kular stood beside Fortune while Nathan, Taltus, Norland, and Theus stood near Swordman. The two teams staring each other down. Kent crouched in the corner, shivering. Yet, not from chilling winds.

"Kent, what's going on?" Fortune asked.

"He wants to come out. He wants to choose his side."

"His side?" Norland said. "You mean between us and the Protectors?"

"Who else!"

Kent ran outside into the field and fell to the ground. Quaking as his body enlarged and the Beast was out. The heroes went out to calm him as his roar terrified the farm animals in the distance. Allison remained in the home, looking out through the window. No fear was preset on her face. Only intrigue. The Beast looked at the teams and sighed. The Beast backhanded Taltus and roared toward the Resistance. The Swordman held his sword in hand.

"Don't make me do this."

The Beast walked toward the Protectors and stood by their

side. Fortune understood, staring down Swordman. Taltus flew toward Beast, however, Swordman ceases him before he collides with the Beast.

"What is happening?" Voltage asked.

"Sides are being chosen." Fortune said. "It's part of nature."

"Not now." Swordman said.

"We'll be taking our leave." Fortune said. "Try to figure out your concern, Swordman."

Fortune opened a portal as he and the Protectors take heir leave. The portal closes as Nathan approached Kenari.

"What is your plan?"

"I have a clue Fortune is the cause of today's circumstance." Swordman replied.

"So, we take them head-on?"

"Looks that way."

Nathan nodded.

"That's fair. I have something I've been working on for a while now. Looks like now's the time."

"You're brining it out already?" Swordman questioned. "Is it capable of withstanding his attacks?"

"Only way to find out is in the field."

"Prepare yourself and we'll meet up later."

Taltus and Theus remained with Swordman at his estate while Hawke and Norland went to the nano-bunker. Inside, Nathan handed Norland a pair of gauntlets. Norland looked at them, seeing how they affect his own cryo-abilities.

"When did you make these?"

"After our battle in Retropolis. Felt it was necessary. Call it a gift."

Norland nodded, putting the gauntlets on as they are covered by ice. Nathan approached the closet of the exposits. He stopped at the door, which was much larger in height and size than the other. The door opened, unveiling a larger suit. Norland walked toward Hawke, looking up at the exosuit.

"Is that what I think it is?" Norland asked.

"It is. I call it the *Beasthunter*."

THE RESISTANCE VS. THE PROTECTORS

Fortune, Voltage, and Kular stood inside the Citadel of Enchantment as Huang entered alongside Tom Bradley. The heroes greeted the sorcerers just as Fortune had made his way back from his study, holding a grimoire in his hands.

"I believe I may have found where the Executioner appeared from."

"Executioner?" Huang asked with confusion. "What's going on?"

"We just returned from Kenari Clark's estate." Fortune said. "The Shadow Executioner was there."

"Where is it now?"

"I sent it back into the Shadow Dimension. No worries, it'll be there for sometime. Until someone or something lets it loose again."

"And where is this Kenari Clark?"

"Still at the estate. With the Resistance."

"The Resistance?!" Tom jolted. "You mean you teamed with them again?"

"Not as planned. Just coincidence. Only to stop the Executioner from remaining in this realm."

"Where are they currently?" Huang wondered.

"With Kenari Clark. The Swordman."

"The Swordman?" Huang replied. "So, the Mythological Man

is real?"

"Wait, you didn't know?" Voltage added. "I thought everyone knew The Swordman existed."

"We're not here to discuss his existence. Right now, we need to find out what brought the Executioner out in the first place. It's not natural for it to have appeared on its own."

"What do you propose?" Huang asked. "Another sorcerer at work against us?"

"Maybe it's Sinister Judge?" Tom said. "We haven't seen him in a while."

"It's not Judge. He would've sent his droids out there to stop us rather than face the Executioner."

"Then, we should start looking." Kular said. "Find the source and ends this before it reaches Atlantis."

"We start with this book. The details in here describe ways of summoning entities from the Shadow Dimension into our own. What is written here only permit's a very powerful sorcerer who can achieve such a feat."

"But, mentor," Tom said. "you're the Supreme Enchanter. There can't be any others more powerful than you in the mystic arts."

Fortune turned to Tom with a clear focus in his eyes. Tom understood and only replied with a nod as Fortune returned to the grimoire. Huang gazed around the Citadel slowly. Voltage and Kular also began to feel something around them. Tom looked up from the book, sensing the energy and Fortune had done the same. He closed the book and approached the Citadel doors.

"Someone's here."

The doors burst with a great explosion. Pushing them back across the Citadel floors. Fortune was thrown against the wall, falling to the floor, yet his eyes were set on the entrance. Through the covering debris, Fortune twirled his hand, clearing the area of the smoke, revealing Nano Man in the much larger exosuit.

"What is that?" Huang pointed.

"It's called the Beasthunter." Nano Man said. "And it's only here for one of you."

"No. No." Kent yelled as he fell to the ground, transforming into the Beast without haste.

"There he is." Nano Man said.

The Beast roared, lunging toward Nano Man. His clawed hands inched closer until he was unknowingly swooped in the air by Taltus, who tossed the monster to the outside field. From the sky, Theus rained down lightning. He looked at the Protectors and pointed toward Kular in particular.

"You! You are a king of a kingdom are you not?!"

"I am. What have you done to Atlantis?"

"I have done nothing. However, you have chosen to align yourself with the opposing force. Therefore, I and those of Eragardia consider you and your Atlantean allies, enemies of the Fifteen Realms!"

"Only way to stop me is to kill me." Kular said, slamming his trident.

"Let us battle! A King against a Millennium God!"

Theus and Kular clashed with the war hammer and trident. The Voltage looked around, seeing the beast being double-teamed by Nano Man and Taltus. He jumped toward to assistance, yet was struck by a blue lightning bolt. Voltage fell, seeing shards of ice on his suit. He looked ahead, seeing Norland standing before him with the gauntlets glowing in the fashion of the arctic.

"What was that fro?"

"That is their fight. Not yours."

"Step aside, Commander. I do not want to hurt you."

"You won't hurt me. You couldn't."

The Voltage flipped himself from the ground, into the air above Norland. The Commander turned swiftly before being hit by a punch from Voltage. Another punch came from the opposite angle as Voltage continued attacking Norland. He shook off the blows before snatching Voltage's arm and clotheslining him to the ground.

"I suggest you stop before this gets worse." Norland warned.

Inside the Citadel, Huang and Tom prepared themselves to join in, however Fortune stepped in front of them, holding his hand.

"Are you sure you don't need our help?" Huang asked.

"Keep this place secure. The Protectors and I will deal with these Resistors."

Huang nodded as he and Tom remained in the Citadel as Fortune exited. He looked out at the fighting before him. Glancing over to his left to see the Beast roared and slamming Taltus just as Nano Man's Beasthunter tackled him to the forest. Fortune looked up, seeing Theus and Kular dueling with their weapons. Fortune turned to his right to see Norland dodging the quickly lighting blasts from Voltage. Fortune sighed.

"I knew you were here as well." Fortune said. "No need to hide."

Fortune turned to see The Swordman standing. His sword in hand while Fortune's hands began to glow. Fortune glanced at Swordman's attire, sensing something peculiar within it. It was much darker than the original suit he wears. This one had no long cloak, only a shorter one which extended to the end of his back.

"What have you done to your suit?"

"This suit was designed simply for those of your kind."

"Ah. One for facing sorcerers."

"You could say that."

"And you believe your sword can withstand my power?"

"It's killed those more powerful than yourself. I suggest you do not tempt the chance."

The wind began to bellow around them as Fortune levitated off the ground. The Swordman kept his eyes on Fortune, not bothered by the supernatural activity around him nor the battle cries and blasts from the others. He clutched the hilt of the sword.

"I guess we're going to find out."

"Before you do, care to give your regards to those you love and trust?"

"Why would I?"

"In case you do not survive this battle."

"I always knew you were no good."

"No. those who practice magic are the ones who are truly evil."

"Enough of this talk!"

Fortune waved his hands as the mystical energy covered them. Swordman raised up his sword just as energy blasts emitted from Fortune's hands. Swordman swiped the blasts out of his way, running towards the Supreme Enchanter with force. Fortune went to twirl once more, yet, Swordman speared Fortune from the air to the ground and started punching Fortune in the face. Fortune blocked the next punch, making his body completely transparent and raising up from beneath Swordman to standing behind him. Swordman turned around and Fortune grabbed him with his mystic power, holding him in the air. Swordman attacked his surroundings, discovering there was an invisible shield around him. He looked down as Fortune kept him in the air.

"He thinks he's clever. I have something for him."

Swordman looked at his right forearm, swiping the inner part, revealing a small capsule. He took the capsule and tossed it against the shield, which let out a bolt of electricity that traveled down to Fortune. Fortune stumbled from the electric shock, looking up to regain himself, Swordman punched atop him, holding him down and the sword against his neck.

"Do make me do it."

Swordman stared into Fortune's eyes and without a thought, he saw something move past them both. Swordman stood up, backing away from Fortune. Fortune rose up, confused as Swordman looked out, seeing the others fighting. He looked back toward Fortune while sheathing the sword.

"What are you doing?" Fortune questioned. "You had me."

"Something's wrong. This is all a ploy."

"What do you mean?"

"Focus." Swordman said, "Humor me. Focus on the surrounding and tell me you aren't sensing it either."

Fortune took Swordman's words seriously and stood still. His hands out and his eyes closed. Fortune began to mediate n the field, muting out the sounds of the continuing battles of the heroes and only hearing silence. Within the silence, Fortune caught the faint sound of laughter. A voice he's only heard some time ago. Fortune's eyes opened widely, he turned toward Swordman.

"What have you found?"

"We've been fooled." fortune replied. "All of this. The Executioner. The strange hatred and anger we've felt since then. The mystery surrounding your estate. It's all part of their plan."

"Who's plan?"

Fortune's eyes shifted above them, keen onto something hidden in plain sight.

"Theirs."

Swordman turned around and looked upward himself. In the air, he saw two figures hidden in the sunlight. He raised his sword and swiped into the air, causing the slashing to impact the figures, revealing themselves. The other heroes paused their fighting, looking toward the figures as well.

"It's about time you figured it out."

The heroes were staring at Noldar and another entity. Dressed in a darker green armor resembling a reptilian with a helmet as high as a top hat. Fortune's hands emitted energy once more, but he was not concerned about Noldar. His focus was on the other as was his own.

"I see the Doctor is still alive after all."

"I can say the same about you. Celd."

IV

A TRICKSTER'S WAYS

The Resistance and Protectors stood side-by-side facing
Noldar and Celd as they descended to the ground. Theus stepped
forward, aiming his war hammer toward Noldar. Noldar extended
his arms with a dark grin.

"How did you escape?!" Theus yelled.

"I have my allies, Millennium God. Just as you do yours."

"Very well, I will send you back. This time with a stronger
force."

"I think not." Celd said, blasting Theus with a stream of
glowing energy.

Theus fell back, rolling on the ground. Nano Man turned,
lunging the Beasthunter toward Celd. Celd waved his hand,
shoving Nano Man aside and crashing to the ground. Voltage,
Norland, Kular, and Beast went in for an attack, but were unable
to match Celd's powerful strength. The only two standing were
Swordman and Fortune. Celd saw and applauded.

"These cannot be the same ones you've spoken about."

"They are. But, today they've learned what it means to face a
true powerful force."

"Indeed. Now, what shall we do with Fortune and this
swordsman."

Noldar stared at the two. Swordman was prepared for the fight
as was Fortune, whose cloak was moving with the wind. Noldar

nodded.

"You can have the sorcerer. I'll take the swordsman."

Celd nodded and immediate attacked Fortune wither energy
blasts. Celd flew off in the air with Fortune following. Swordman
and Noldar took across from each other. Their eyes were locked
on. Noldar chuckled as Swordman twirled his sword. Noldar
nodded.

"Not bad. Although, I must warn you. This will not end like
last time."

"Last I checked, we didn't exactly have a confrontation
between us. You were too busy either running or dealing with
Theus."

"That won't happen this time."

Swordman nodded as Noldar rushed toward him with the
spear head-on. Swordman dodged the coming attack and slammed
his sword atop Noldar's spear. The impact trembled the ground
beneath their feet, knocking them both to the ground as the
shockwave jolted the other heroes as they began to awake on the
ground. Taltus arose, seeing Swordman blocking the attacks from
Noldar. He looked up, seeing Fortune and Celd firing energy
toward each other. Taltus flew with speed, spearing Noldar. Kular
and Voltage jumped up, seeing Fortune.

"I got this." Kular said, throwing his trident in the air.

Celd turned back, seeing the trident and catching it. He held
it and measured its weight. Celd chuckled.

"This is Atlantean material?!"

Celd turned back, looking down at Kular and launched the
trident back to him. Kular caught the trident as Celd's own
strength caused it to stick into the ground, pushing Kular
backwards. Voltage looked up and fired several lightning blasts
toward Celd. All of them he deflected with his own energy.
Fortune conjured several spheres and tossed them toward Celd,
only for him to turn them toward Voltage, who moved out of

their path as they exploded behind him, filling the grounds with shards of electricity.

"This guy is powerful." Voltage said.

Norland walked forward. His gauntlets charged up as he swiped his arm, letting out a blast of cold lightning. The electric blast made its mark on Celd's back. Shocking him slightly as he shook off the jolts. He turned, looking down toward Norland. He grinned.

"The cold does not harm one like myself!"

"How about a titagod." Taltus said, coming from behind Celd, punching him in the face.

Celd fell to the ground with Fortune following. Taltus flew back and forth between Noldar and Celd. Giving them damage only he could achieve at such a speed. Swordman stood back as Taltus took down Noldar, shattering his spear. Theus arose and threw his hammer at Noldar, knocking him into the wilderness. Celd stood up, dusting himself off from the blow. He turned around, seeing Fortune charged up with mystic energy, Voltage standing ready, Kular aiming his trident, Norland holding his ground. From behind Celd arrived the Beast and the Beasthunter. Celd was surrounded as Swordman, Taltus, and Theus dealt with Noldar. Celd let out a short sigh.

"This is not what he pictured."

"You're done, Celd." Fortune proclaimed. "This mind game you've set up is over."

"Perhaps it is." Celd smirked. "Yet, the war is yet to begin."

Celd evaporated into little pieces of energy which floated into the air and vanished. Fortune looked at the others and gave a slight nod. They turned around, seeing Theus having Noldar's hands in chains. Voltage pointed.

"Where'd you get the chains?"

"Eragardian magic has its uses." Theus replied. "Noldar knows them well."

"Too well." Fortune said. "So, this is done."

"For now." Noldar said. "The war is coming."

"What war?" Fortune wondered.

"He's coming. Don't you feel it, sorcerer? The skies will open once again. Only this time, you and your allies will not be able to stop the coming takeover."

"Who's he?" Fortune asked.

Taltus stood back, hearing Noldar's words. His mind began to wander.

"You'll find out soon. All of you will!"

"Alright." Theus said. "I'll take him back to Eragard. See all of again some other time."

Theus raised his hammer as a lighting bolt came down and took him and Noldar from the earth. The heroes gathered themselves as Fortune and Swordman sat inside the Citadel. Discussing their own terms in agreement. The two decided if what Noldar and Celd are saying to be true, they will unite together. Resistance and Protectors to face the threat. The Beast however remains with the Protectors, no longer referring himself as a member of the Resistance.

Elsewhere, far from the earth. A hooded man covered in gothic-style robe stood in the midst of a misty landscape. The stench of burning flesh covered the air. Behind the man appeared a much larger figure standing in the doorway to which only his massive size could be seen as were his glowing eyes.

"Is it prepared?" The tall figure asked.

"As you've wished. Noldar rand Celd have done their part. The heroes have collided, and are unsure of what's next."

"Very good. Prepare the Ophfiends. The invasion is nigh."

I

RESISTANCE MISSION

During the day, the Outband make themselves public, using the technology they've been smuggling for months. While making an attempt to smuggle more tech inside an warehouse nearly close to Enigma City, Taltus flew down in front of them, startling them as some remember their last encounter.

"Where's Bontade?" Taltus asked.

"Why would we tell you?" One of the men said. "You're in our way!"

"I'm not going anywhere. Neither are you."

"Or what?"

"Don't trigger him, man." Another man said.

"Or what? He's gong to kill us like he did those other guys?"

"I did not kill them. They still live. However, you aren't like them. So, I will give you this choice to surrender before you make a mistake."

"Just get out of our way."

Taltus nodded.

"Suit yourselves."

Taltus flew up into the air as the Outband watched. They glanced down in front of them, seeing The Swordman and Commander Norland standing in between them and the warehouse. The appearance of Swordman terrified the Outband and they took off, running back to their van. Inching closer, the van exploded due to a large lightning bolt, which bolted down from above. They glanced up to the sky expecting to see Taltus, however, it was Theus himself.

"Shit! It's them!"

"You're done here." Norland said.

"Where's the other guy?" The Outband said to each other. "He's supposed to be here."

"Who are you talking about?" Swordman questioned.

"Wouldn't you like to know."

Swordman quickly threw a shuriken toward the man, knocking the gun from his hand. The man jolted with a yell, grabbing his hand tightly as the shuriken sliced his hand before piercing into the gun.

"Where is Bontade?" Taltus asked again, hovering down in front of them.

"He's going to get help."

"Help? What kind of help?"

Above them rained down several cars, surprising the Resistance. Taltus flew up, catching one of the vehicles and placing it on the ground. The Outband ran off as in the distance, Taltus looked and pointed.

"There's Bontade."

"And who's the other guy?" Theus asked.

They looked out, seeing Bontade was not alone. Beside him was a much larger man. Both in height and stature. His physique was nearly the same size as the Beast. Theus stepped forward as Bontade applauded their presence.

"I wasn't' expecting heroes to be witnesses to my operations."

"You've seemed to have forgotten what I told you." Taltus said. "Your manufacturing days are over."

"Yes, they are done. But not how you're thinking. The work is finished. He is on his way."

"Who's on their way?" Swordman asked.

"You will all know very soon."

Swordman held out his sword, with the tip set nearly against Bontade's throat. The much larger man roared, backhanding Swordman from Bontade. Taltus flew and tackled him with a spear, pushing him back. However, the man was strong enough to withstand Taltus' strength and grabbed him by his head, planting him in the ground. Theus grinned as lightning formed on his hands.

"Leave this one to me, comrades."

"I'll take Bontade." Swordman replied.

"I'll help the others with the Outband." Taltus responded, flying off toward Norland.

Theus levitated in the air as Bontade ran off with Swordman chasing him. The larger man stood his ground, pouncing his fists and stomping.

"Before we fight, what is your name?" Theus asked.

"I am Mane."

"Mane? Never heard of you before. You must be new around here."

"Enough of this prattle talk!"

"Very well." Theus replied, striking Mane with a lightning blast.

Mane stumbled in his steps as the lightning pierced his body. Theus held his stance as the lightning flowed from his hands. Mane stretched out his hand against the lightning, pushing it back. Theus noticed the tactic.

"Ah! A challenge!"

Theus reached to his back, raising up his war hammer, Mithrandir. He raises the hammer, connecting its own energy with the lightning. Above Mane conjured a tornado, which only encompass the area around him and Theus. Over on the other side, Taltus and Norland take out the Outband with ease as Bontade runs into the building, attempting to hide from The

Swordman. Scrambling around several cargo crates as Swordman walked through the room silently.

"I know you're here." Swordman said. "Do yourself the favor and ends this."

Bontade exhaled heavily, reaching down near one of the cargo crates, grabbing a crowbar. He gripped the crowbar tightly. Exhaling once more before bolting out from the crates toward Swordman.

"You won't take me alive!" Bontade screamed.

Swordman moved to the side, avoiding the crowbar. Bontade turned around, only to receive a punch from Swordman and he fell to the floor. Swordman shook his head, placing his sword in its sheath.

"That was simple."

Theus and Mane continue battling. This time with punches. Theus delivered several blows mixed with lighting blasts while Mane used his fists and head to attack Theus. Theus raises his hammer once more and throws it at Mane, clashing him in the chest and pushing him further from the warehouse. The hammer returns to Theus as he placed it away. He looked ahead as Taltus and Norland walked toward him.

"Is he done?" Norland asked.

Theus looked out, seeing Mane's silhouette ahead. He can tell he's running. Theus nodded with a grin.

"He's still coming."

"I'll take this one." Taltus said.

Taltus stood still as Mane ran toward them with a much greater speed than average. Mane screamed as his fists went first. Taltus dodged the blow and delivered a much larger blow to Mane, punching him in the face and chest before grabbing him by his throat and tossing him to the ground. Taltus descended, seeing that Mane was finished.

"You didn't kill him did you?" Norland asked.

"No. He's very much alive. Just sleeping."

Afterwards, a dozen T.I.T.A.N. agents arrived at the warehouse, confiscating the technology. Swordman and Nano Man spoke with several of them detailing the events which took place while Taltus escorted Bontade and Mane to the T.I.T.A.N. truck, taking them to a secure facility. The truck drives off as Theus approached Taltus.

"It seems this Mane fellow was somewhat of a challenge."

"What makes you say that?" Taltus asked.

"For starters, it's a shame Brock wasn't here for this. The Beast would've loved to face Mane one-on-one. A worthy adversary to his feats."

"Perhaps."

Later in the day, Kenari went to visit Hawke in his nano-bunker. While there, Nathan continued working on several exposits as well as repairing the Beasthunter armor, which he states he will wear again. The two discussed the recent events concerning the Outband and Mane. Their conversation had turned toward Bontade's words. They confused Nathan, yet, Kenari was on to something.

"What did Taltus think of it?" Hawke asked.

"From what I could tell, he knows something about all of this. He's dealt with the Outband before. He might know who they're working for."

"True. Should ask him tomorrow."

"I was going to do that." Kenari replied. "Meanwhile, I might as well confirm there's something heading toward us from above."

"Again? Like what?"

"I'm not sure. It's readings are similar to King Stroh's entry, yet, much stronger and cryptic."

"I know what's coming." said a voice from behind Kenari and Nathan.

They both turned with haste, only to see Taltus sanding at the entrance of the bunker. He nodded while looking around at the suits. He smirked.

"I know you weren't expecting me."

"Yeah." Nathan shrugged. "I wasn't."

"You heard everything we said so far?" Kenari asked.

"I did and I can tell you what's coming."

"Well, what is coming?" Hawke wondered. "Another invasion?"

"Not just an invasion. A takeover."

"From who?" Kenari asked.

"Oranos."

II

BLACHOLIAN INVADERS

The next day, Hawke went to his headquarters for an executive meeting, primarily reflecting on the past events concerning Giovanni Marko's idea of biotechnology. Hawke disagreed with his partners in using the tech for a much larger scale. Alice Jacobs sat beside him, monitoring the meeting. She glanced at the boardroom table, seeing the diagrams of Marko's. Hawke looked to her, seeing her eyes locked on the diagram. He reached over, picking them up.

"What is it?"

"Why does his diagrams look like the suits?"

"Because he was making his own. Or making a suit. I only saw one."

While they chatted, a loud bang echoed throughout the city, shattering the windows of the buildings near its sound. The glass fell atop the civilians as they ran for cover. The bang reached the headquarters, only shaking the building. Hawke paused as the others began to fear. Believing it to have been an earthquake. Hawke told them it couldn't have been, due to the fact of the bang originating from the sky. The sky cracked open as the clouds above moved aside, giving way to a large portal, glowing in such a beautiful colors, yet pulsing with energy at every second. From the portal came down a figure, covered in a dark-gold armor from head to toe. The figure wielded a staff made of the same armor material. From the headquarters, Hawke and Alice stood by the window, looking out toward the city, seeing the portal and the descending figure. Hawke sighed and Alice knew what was coming next.

"I have no choice." Hawke said. "Keep them occupied, will you."

Hawke exited the headquarters, raising his hands into the air after pressing a button on his watch. In the distance, flying toward Hawke was the Nano Man armor. Making its landing directly in front of him, Hawke placed on the armor and headed out toward the city. Hawke flew into the downtown area of Newark, glancing up at the portal, which is still pulsing. Inside of it Hawke could only see a bright light with some shades of a darker force behind it. He looked down at the streets, seeing the golden-clad figure. His A.I. caught the staff, measuring its energy.

"The staff is imbued with some kind of ancient power source."

"Thanks, CARDELL." Hawke said. "Anything else I should know about it?"

"Well, for starters, the staff is made of the same material the Outband was smuggling out."

"Is that a fact." Hawke chuckled. "This must've been the guy Taltus told us about. I'll ask him."

Nano Man landed in front of the figure, gaining its attention. Hawke realized how tall the figure was and nodded.

"He's a big guy."

"What is this?" The armored one said. "A being made of metal."

"Not exactly. Who are you and why are you here?"

"I am Thrudhawk, General of Blachole."

"Ok. What's with the goat horns?"

"This is the time of Oranos."

"Oranos. Where is he then?"

"He's on his way. Right now, he's sent me to take out any

adversaries who may stand in his way."

"I see and have you found any so far?"

"Just one."

Thrudhawk slammed the staff into the road, trembling the ground and stumbling Nano Man in his steps. Trying to maintain his balance, Nano Man hovered into the air, only to have his leg grabbed by Thrudhawk, who proceeded to slam him into the road and tossing him through one of the nearby buildings.

"Where's the Titagod?" Thrudhawk asked.

"You mean Taltus?" Nano Man replied. "Oh, he's around. Just not here."

"Oh. He will show up. He's on my list."

"That's nice."

Nano Man blasted Thrudhawk with his energy beans, flying from the building and around the armored one. Striking him with every energy beam. Thrudhawk twirled the staff, deflecting the beams as he held it still and firing a beam back at Nano Man, collapsing him on the ground. Thrudhawk chuckled as he walked toward the Nano Man, dragging the staff on the ground slowly. The scratching echo irritated Hawke.

"Best I move you out of my way." Thrudhawk said. "Another martyr for the worlds to cry for."

Thrudhawk raised the staff above Nano Man. Slamming it down, only for the staff to impale into the concrete next to Nano Man's body. He looked around and Thrudhawk was gone. The sounds around him moved as the wind blew. Up ahead, Hawke could see Taltus holding Thrudhawk in the distance before slamming him in the ground and returning to him. Taltus stood above Nano Man and extended his hand, helping him.

"Thanks for coming."

"I was in the area after I felt the energy coming from that portal."

"He asked about you." Nano Man said. "I guess you two have

a history."

"A short one."

Taltus and Nano Man stood side by side as Thrudhawk walked toward them. He faced the two heroes, wiping the blood from his face as he let out a laugh.

"What's funny?" Nano Man asked.

"You thought this would be a two-on-one battle?"

The portal sparked, gaining their attention. They looked up and saw another figure coming down, only this one was much larger in size than Thrudhawk, but a tad bit shorter.

"The hell is that?" Nano Man asked.

"Dominix." Taltus replied.

"How do you know these guys?"

"It's a complicated situation."

Dominix came down and walked beside Thrudhawk. His eyes were locked on Taltus, never made even a slight glance toward Nano Man. Thrudhawk could sense the energy between Taltus and Dominix and chuckled. He nodded.

"I see. I will take the metal one."

"Much appreciated." Dominix replied.

III

THE COMING OF ORANOS

Dominix roared and ran toward Taltus, spearing him down the street as Thrudhawk lunged at Nano Man with the staff. Nano Man flew from the coming attack and fired several rounds of miniature missiles, which Thrudhawk deflected. Taltus continued being shoved by Dominix and slammed his feet into the concrete, ceasing Dominix's strength. Taltus grinned as he snatched him by his hair and slammed him repeatedly. Taltus gazed up to the sky, seeing the portal was still open. He retuned is focus to Dominix, who quickly uppercut him, stumbling his steps. Dominix roared again as he held Taltus by the throat and throwing him back into the streets of Newark.

Nano Man continued firing rounds toward Thrudhawk, who only laughed while deflecting them with his staff. Nano Man shrugged his shoulders, holding out his hands, releasing more energy beams. Thrudhawk pushed through the beams and swiped Nano Man from the air with the staff, causing him to crash into the road. Next to him fell Taltus by Dominix's throw. The two heroes looked at each other while Thrudhawk and Dominix walked toward them both. Laughing.

"We're not enough." Nano Man said.

"We can take them." Taltus replied. "I've done it before."

"At the same time?"

Taltus nodded with a sigh.

"Contact the others. Tell them what's happening."

"Already have." Nano Man said.

Thrudhawk stopped his steps while Dominix continued approaching Taltus. Thrudhawk slammed his staff into the ground, startling Dominix. He turned back toward him, seeing the serious expression on Thrudhawk's face.

"We can take them out now." Dominix said.

"No. Oranos specifically demanded we keep the titagod alive."

"But, he is our adversary. Oranos' adversary. He could ruin all of his plans."

"That's an order."

Thrudhawk raised the staff, turning back and looking at the portal. He raised the staff, pointing it at the portal, which released another shock wave. Only this time what emerged from the portal were the Ophfiends. The legions of Blachole. Taltus saw them in hordes as the flew over Newark. Nano Man sighed heavily, seeing the creature above his city.

"The hell is happening here?" Nano Man questioned.

"Once the others are here, we can finish this." Taltus replied. "No concern to us."

The ophfiends surrounded Taltus and Nano Man while Thrudhawk held his staff above his head and Dominix roared. Taltus kept his eyes on Thrudhawk while feeling the blowing winds from the ophfiends' wings.

"Anytime now." Nano Man whispered.

Behind Thrudhawk let out a loud horn. The two Blacholians turned around, seeing a series of T.I.T.A.N. convoys with agents bolting out of the doors. Alongside them were Agents Mariah Cooper, Jessica Mara. Also with them were the Champions and Lady Siren. From the last convoy exited colonel Evan Nader, who quickly saw the two Blacholians and shook his head while gazing in up at the portal.

"This again."

"Reinforcements." Thrudhawk smirked. "They want an even battle."

"Let us take them." Dominix said. "Rid of the rodents while Lord Oranos deals with the titagod."

Thrudhawk nodded. Slamming his staff as Dominix and the ophfiends went for the agents. The Agents began firing their rounds at the flying creatures while Dominix bolted toward them like a wild bull. Smashing the convoys in front of him. Taltus and Nano Man saw the shooting while Taltus kept his focus on Thrudhawk.

"I'll take him." Taltus said.

"Wait."

Taltus flew into the air, tackling Thrudhawk into the roads, pummeling him as several ophfiends move behind him, clawing at his neck. Taltus swiped them away as Thrudhawk arose and swiped the titagod with the staff. Taltus fell back as Thrudhawk jumped over his body, holding the staff at his chest. Nano Man raised up, but was only knocked down by three ophfiends.

"You fool." Thrudhawk said. "This is not like our last encounter."

"I am aware. This time you won't return to Blachole alive."

"You really believe that?"

"I've already spoken it."

Thrudhawk sighed, raising up the staff. Preparing to impale Taltus. However, a blast of ice lightning sparked the staff, knocking it from Thrudhawk's hands. He looked around for the source, only to find himself staring at Commander Norland. Behind him were Bionic Rage, Q-Arrow, John Terror, and Nonagon. The heroes ran to the aid of Taltus and Nano Man, firing shots at Thrudhawk and the ophfiends.

"More of them!" Thrudhawk yelled.

"Rage! Terror!" Norland yelled. "Go and help the agents. Arrow. Nonagon. You're with me."

Rage flew toward the agents, firing his armed machine rounds at the ophfiends. Terror moved into the fight, firing shots as well alongside slashing the ophfiends with his sword. Norland moved toward Taltus and Nano Man as Arrow and Nonagon entered the fight against Thrudhawk.

"I wasn't aware of the new guy joining in." Nano Man said.

"Nonagon had to do something besides sit around the headquarters all day." Norland replied.

"Where's Kenari?" Taltus asked.

"He's on his way." Norland said, pointing above them in the sky.

They looked up and saw the Sky-Rapier hovering above them and The Swordman slid down from the craft. The Sky-Rapier flew off as Swordman approached them calmly in the midst of the ongoing battle. The Swordman scouted the area, seeing the agents, the ophfiends, and Thrudhawk in front of them.

"Who's the horned one?" Swordman asked.

"Thrudhawk." Taltus replied. "One of Oranos' lieutenants."

"One." Norland said. "Where are the others?"

"One's over near the agents. Dominix."

"I see Rage and Terror have their hands full." Nano Man said. "Also, where's Theus?"

Thrudhawk ran toward them and before he could raise the staff, the war hammer Mithrandir appeared spearing Thrudhawk to the ground. The hammer returned to Theus, who was standing behind the heroes in the middle of their talk. Theus nodded.

"I see I came on good timing."

Thrudhawk rose up, seeing The Resistance. He shrugged off the attack and stood his ground, repeatedly slamming his staff to get their attention. They turned and saw him glaring as he twirled the staff.

"Five of you. This is a battle to be had."

"Give it up, Thrudhawk." Taltus said. "You're outnumbered."

"Am I?"

Six ophfiends moved like eagles, hurling down from above at the Resistance. Clashing with them while Thrudhawk jumped into the battle, swiping his staff against Theus' hammer. Taltus snatched Thrudhawk by his goat horns and blasted him with his lightning vision while Theus smashed the hammer into Thrudhawk's chest. Swordman slashed his way through one of the ophfiends while Norland, Nano Man, and Nonagon handled the others.

On the other end, Rage ran into battle with Dominix. Seeing how the Blacholian surpassed him in height, it was a challenge for the Marine. He jerked his arms, which began to click and he raised them toward Dominix, firing several rounds of grenades. Dominix stumbled back as the grenades exploded in his face. Wiping the smoke from is sight, Terror jumped up, slashing him in his chest with his sword.

While the Resistance fought Thrudhawk and the ophfiends, another portal began to open nearby. The Swordman saw the colors, knowing it wasn't another Blacholian portal. It was magic. From the portal arrived the Protectors, who joined in on the battle. Thrudhawk looked up, seeing the Beast running toward him as he snatched him by his horns and tossed him into one of the nearby windows with ease. Doctor Fortune approached Swordman. The two looked at one another sternly, then they nodded.

"Wasn't expecting you here." Swordman said.

"I sensed the portal's energy. Therefore, I had to arrive."

The Voltage and Kular moved into the fight, joining in with Rage and Terror against Dominix. The Beast continued pummeling Thrudhawk into the ground with his fists and feet. The Resistance looked around as they continued taking out the ophfiends. As the battle continued, Taltus caught the sudden urge to gaze into the sky at the portal. He could sense something and it was strong. Fortune also sensed the same energy as he looked up. Thrudhawk double-kicked the Beast from near him as he flipped himself to his feet, looking at the portal. He grinned. Swordman looked at Taltus and Fortune, seeing their eyes were set on the portal.

"What is it?" Swordman asked Taltus.

"Oranos is here."

The fighting went still as everyone looked up at the entrance of Oranos. The intimidating entity moved through the sky, coming down from the portal. All of the ophfiends were in awe, immediately kneeling. Dominix and Thrudhawk followed. Their eyes were set to the ground as Oranos landed in between them. He measured everyone from the T.I.T.A.N. agents to the heroes. He looked to his right and saw Taltus. He grinned.

"I told you this day would come, titagod."

"This world isn't yours." Taltus replied.

"Oh, it is. Because I say so."

"Who gave you the authority to traverse between realms?" Fortune asked.

"I command myself."

"You have no authority to be here." Swordman said. "Best you leave."

"I see the titagod has found himself some allies. Good. All will suit well within my army."

"We're not joining your army." Norland said, stepping forward. "I suggest you take your lieutenants and soldiers and leave this place."

"Such fire within you all." Oranos smiled. "All the better for what must be done."

Oranos turned around to Thrudhawk. He commanded for him to rise up and stand. Thrudhawk followed the orders as he approached his master. Oranos nodded while looking at the ophfiends and Dominix in the distance.

"Return to Blachole." Oranos commanded.

"Are you sure you do not need our assistance against these peasants?"

"I will handle them myself. Tell Dagard to prepare all necessary duties to ensure our victory."

"Yes, my master."

Thrudhawk rallied the ophfiends as he did Dominix and they flowed above into the portal. Once they entered, the portal closed, startling the heroes. Oranos moved to the side as the Resistance stood with the Protectors and the other heroes. The agents followed suit, moving alongside them. On one end of the road were the heroes of earth. On the other was Oranos. All alone.

"It's just you against us." Taltus said. "You will not win this."

"Won't I? Let us test that boast."

Swordman held his sword as the others prepared themselves. Lightning emitting from Theus' hands. The Beast roared greatly as Kular tapped his trident and Fortune levitated from the ground as did Taltus. The agents were prepared with their guns loaded. Oranos stood still. His hands to his side with only a sinister grin on his face.

"Let's finish this." Taltus said.

In one swoop, they all rushed toward Oranos. Attacking him with everything they had in their possession. Oranos did not make a move and only shielded himself with a energy field. Not even Fortune's magic could break through the shield. Swordman ran toward Oranos and impale the sword into the shield, cracking it. Oranos saw the crack and looked at Swordman. The shield went down as he kicked Swordman from him. Taltus flew at Oranos with three punches, Theus attacked with his lightning and hammer. The others followed and yet it wasn't enough. Oranos blasted them all with a large wave of Helvish energy. The blast of the energy was powerful enough to take out all of the agents, Nader included. The Voltage moved with speed to attack Oranos and he was suddenly snatched in mid-air and stomped into the ground. Kular dove down with his trident against Oranos and it was not enough. Oranos' own speed surpassed Kular as he took him down. The Beast rushed toward him with punches, kicks, and spears. However, Oranos' own strength was able to outmatch the Beast as he attacked him with several punches before raising him up and slamming him into the other heroes.

"You've proven useless to me." Oranos said, turning his back on them.

"Where are you going!" Taltus yelled, flying towards Oranos.

Oranos looked back and caught Taltus in the air, holding him by his throat, strangling him. The Resistance went into assistance, u they were knocked back by Oranos' negonic beams. Taltus struggled to fight back as Oranos grinned.

"You see, titagod. Your world isn't much for long. I will return with my might and then, this world shall be mine."

Oranos dropped Taltus as he opened another portal and walked through. Taltus saw the portal and Oranos. He stood up with haste. Swordman saw him and knew what he was about to do. He stood up as did the others, including the Protectors.

"NO!" Taltus flew into the portal.

"We have to follow him." Swordman said. "Now!"

The ones who followed Taltus into the portal were Swordman, Nano Man, Norland, Theus, Fortune, Voltage, and Kular. The portal closed behind them. Leaving Rage, Terror, Arrow, and Nonagon to remain with the downed agents. Nonagon looked around, seeing only the destructive power of the Blacholians and the might of Oranos.

"Save this world." Nonagon said. "For the chosen's fate."

IV

A TITAGOD VS. A DARK GOD

Through a brightly dimensional wormhole, the Resistance and Protectors made their way into Blachole. Seeing its darkly appearance gave out a sense of dread. The portal sealed as they stepped foot on Blacholian ground. The Swordman looked around, not seeing Taltus anywhere. Fortune circled the area as they looked up toward the molten castle, seeing a large statue of Oranos standing over them.

"You're sensing what I'm sensing?" Norland asked the team.

"The negative energy?" Fortune answered. "Yeah, we're all sensing it."

"Ugh!" Theus grunted. "Where's Taltus?"

"He's here." Swordman replied, gazing around the rocky exteriors around them. "Somewhere."

The Voltage looked ahead down the pathway leading to the castle. In the distance he could make out several figures moving. He pointed in the direction.

"Perhaps he went that way."

"We're going anyway." Swordman replied. "I hope everyone is prepared for the fight that's coming."

"We are." Kular said.

The Beast let out a roar as he charged down the pathway toward the moving figures. As the Beast inched closer, he saw them to be Blacholian guards wielding staves. The Beast bolted through them like nothing, smashing them against the walls and the ground, cracking it beneath his feet. The Beast continued moving as the others followed, seeing the downed guards.

"He's useful." Theus said.

"When he needs to be." Nano Man added.

"Very much so." Swordman replied. "Let's see where Taltus went off to."

The Beast fought off several more guards before finding himself surrounded by more ophfiends. Screeching and clawing their way at the Beast, he backhands a pair of them with one arm before stomping the ground, causing a shockwave to knock down the others around him. The Beast looked ahead, seeing two large doors nearly twenty feet in height. The Beast approached the doors, punching them with all his might. The others reached the doors and the Swordman paused the Beast, taking a moment to examine the door. He raised his sword and slashed it against the door.

"It isn't any know metal I'm familiar with." Nano Man said, scouting the material. "It's not even close to quakerium or solidium."

"Must be made from the minerals here and only here." Fortune replied. "Either way, we need to get these doors open."

The Beast returned punching the door as Theus and Kular aided him with their own weapons. The door showed no signs of damage and The Beast stepped back and rammed the doors with his shoulder. No effect on the doors. The Beast went for it once again and this time nothing happened. Fortune conjured a large mystical disc of energy and tossed it against the door. The door shook from the magic, yet did not bulge. Fortune sighed. Nano Man charged up, shooting several energy beams from his hands. No effect.

"I'm not understanding the physics of this place."

"It's not from earth." Norland said.

"So, I'm just curious." Voltage spoke. "we're in another dimension? Like a whole 'nother place?"

"Yes." Fortune said.

"Strange place indeed." Nano Man said. "Since this place is real, there must be others. Countless others."

"There are." Fortune answered. "Best not to contact them. Some of them aren't very friendly of strangers. Particularly the humankind."

"And our only way back is finding Taltus and defeating Oranos." Swordman added. "That is why we need to get through these doors."

"You have something in mind?" Fortune asked Swordman.

"Like blasting through those doors?" Nano Man said.

"What did you have in mind?"

"After you."

Swordman nodded. "All together now."

Kular twirled his trident as Theus conjured his own power into his hammer. Norland smashed his fists together, forming icy on the gauntlets. The Beast charged himself up as Voltage did the same. Nano Man charged up his chest for the blast. Fortune surrounded himself with a magic barrier as Swordman held his sword in a steady position. All of them faced the doors and together, they let out an attack, hitting the doors with all their might. Then, a clicking sound echoed through the pathway as the doors slowly opened with a enduring creak.

"Appears to have worked." Voltage said. "Now, what's next?"

"We find Taltus." Swordman said.

"What of Oranos' forces. The ones we encounter in Newark? Plus, the others whom we have yet to meet?"

"We'll deal with them when the time comes." Swordman answered.

They walked through the doors. Seeing much of Blachole in itself. Surrounding them were lava falls and purging flames.

Smoke did not cover the air above them. Swordman looked around, seeing the tall statue of Oranos and near it stood other statures, smaller in scale. They were statues of Thrudhawk, Dominix, and two others they were not familiar with. Looking ahead, Swordman caught something moving in the air with speed. The fainted color of blue passed over.

"There's Taltus."

"Where?" Fortune asked, looking around.

"He went into the castle."

Looking straight ahead, they see the cathedral doors opening and they make their move toward them. Coming closer, they see the massive stairs in front of them. Measuring at almost three feet in height. They reached the doors and entered the castle. The interior covered with illustrated stained glass windows depicting images of Blacholian figures and symbols. Inside, they saw Taltus in the distance flying and he stopped in mid-air. Hovering above a set of doors. Three of them. Each one with a different feature. The left had an image of a goat-horned figure. The middle featured the mark of Helven. The right detailed a flaming furnace.

"Something's not right in here." Fortune said.

"I know." Swordman replied.

"Now, what's the plan?" Voltage asked.

"Can you reach him?" Swordman asked Theus.

"I'll do my best."

Theus hovered and flew toward Taltus. Approaching him, Theus is quickly taken down by a surprising force of ophfiends. From the castle windows emerged more ophfiends and the doors in front of Taltus and Theus opened, causing them to move back toward the others. Taltus regrouped as they found themselves surrounded and outnumbered. The heroes were ready for the fight as the screeches of the ophfiends echoed loudly in the castle. Entering from the doors were Thrudhawk, Dominix, and another figure. This one cloaked in a hood, dressed in a robe. He raised his arms and applauded the heroes' arrival.

"Lord Oranos will be pleased you've arrived."

"Where is he?!" Taltus yelled.

"Where he's occupied is not your business to know, titagod."

"I take it you're close to this Oranos." Norland said. "You must be his servant."

"I am Dagard. Mercenary and Preacher of Blachole."

"This place has a preacher?" Kular said.

"Everything has something to worship." Swordman answered.

Thrudhawk stepped forward, aiming his staff toward the heroes. Dominix began to salivate as he saw them. Itching for the attack. Dagard sensed the tension and he enjoyed it. Every moment. He clapped his hands and the ophfiends went in for the attack. The heroes spread themselves to combat the flying forces. Thrudhawk and Dominix jumped into the fight, attacking the heroes from all corners. From there, Dagard stood back near the three doors and watched.

Fortune took out several ophfiends before turning his eyes toward Dagard. Dagard grinned as Fortune was swiped by Thrudhawk's staff. Nano Man flew into the air, blasting the ophfiends around him with his energy beams. Afterwards, Dominix jumped and tackled Nano Man to the marbled floor. Dominix went for a punch, yet, his arm was snatched by the Beast as he tossed him against the concreted wall.

"We need a plan." Swordman said.

"I need to get through one of those doors." Taltus said. "Oranos is somewhere in this place."

"Taltus, let one of us accompany you." Fortune suggested. "That way things can be sorted out well."

"There's no time for that. Oranos personally came to me and I must face him alone."

Swordman looked out as he slashed three ophfiends toward the doors, seeing Dagard still standing in his place. He pointed ahead.

"We'll need to distract him to give you an opening."

"I'm ready." Taltus said.

Swordman turned to Fortune and they agreed with a nod. Norland turned to them both, looking ahead.

"I'll help out."

They were ready and made their move toward the doors. Dagard saw them and yelled, raising his arms to cause the floor to tremble. Taltus flew ahead, punching Dagard as he stopped at the doors. Swordman jumped up, going for an attack on Dagard, who moved swiftly from the sword's impact. Norland let out several blasts of icy lightning, hitting Dagard in the knees while Fortune swiped his mystic discs across Dagard's chest.

"You thought magic would serve you here!" Dagard yelled. "This is a place of darkness!"

Dagard grabbed Fortune by his neck as he kicked both Swordman and Norland from his surroundings. Taltus continued looking at the doors, deciphering which one he should enter. Behind them, Theus and Beast dealt with Thrudhawk as the staff collided with the hammer. The Beast threw several blows to Thrudhawk's abdomen, stumbling the horned one while Theus uppercutted him with the hammer into the air, flying over him and slamming him into the floor with a blast of lightning.

Nano Man, Voltage, and Kular dealt with Dominix and the remaining ophfiends. Nano Man and Voltage combined their power set to attack Dominix while Kular used his trident to impale the hairy one into the floor while swiping it in the air to attack the ophfiends. Dagard continued chocking Fortune as Swordman rose up and went in for another attack, only for Dagard to catch him, grabbing him by the throat with his left hand. Norland ran in for a tackle, yet the tackle didn't move Dagard as he smirked before stomping on Norland's back, holding him to the floor with his foot.

"Such foolish creatures! Do you not know where you are?! This is Blachole! Magic will not help you here nor will you spirituality! Negonic energy rules this domain. Helven is this place's source!"

Taltus paused, hearing Dagard's words. He turned back, seeing the others in a dire situation. Bolting like lighting, Taltus speared Dagard, causing him to drop Swordman and Fortune, giving Norland room to move. Smashing Dagard through one of the windows, Taltus returned to the doors and he nodded.

"Helven."

Taltus pressed the button near the middle door, it opened. Thrudhawk heard the sound, turning back to see Taltus entered the door as the others retuned to the battle, finishing off the ophfiends and facing Dominix. He let out a massive scream as Theus smashed the hammer against his head, shattering one of the horns. The Beast stood over him and pummeling his body into the floor to the point where Thrudhawk was buried nearly three feet into the ground.

Taltus walked through a dark corridor, hearing sounds of the battle echoing behind him. He walked further, finding himself in a throne room. The walls of the room were flowing with magma at every corner. The heat was nearly unbearable. Taltus fully entered the room and in front of him, he saw Oranos sitting on the throne. His hands folded together and s sinister grin on his face.

"You knew I would come."

"Of course. It was only written in the fates of the past."

"Your invasion is not going to happen."

"You seek to stop my actions?"

"Why else would I be here? You threaten all the lives back on Earth. I cannot allow someone like you to conquer it."

"And if I refuse your dire threats?"

"I will have no choice but to finish you off."

Oranos nodded, rising up from the throne. Taltus gripped his fists as he eyes sparked. Oranos' own eyes purged with energy as he moved his arms to his side. Standing calmly before Taltus. The two forces stood opposite of one another. Ready for the fight.

"This is a sight to behold." Oranos said. "A titagod and a dark god. Standing face-to-face. Opposite odds of the cosmos."

"One that will end with your defeat."

"Very well. Any last words before your death?"

"The people of Earth will be spared from the distress of a despot like yourself."

"I am many things, Taltus. If you only knew, would you have changed your mind to coming here. But, anyhow, this day I will take the role as simply, The Destroyer."

Oranos blasted Taltus with his energy beams, knocking the titagod into the magma walls. Taltus shook himself, seeing his chest covered with lava. Wiping it off as he flew toward Oranos, spearing him over his throne seat and across the room. Punching him as he moved. Oranos grabbed Taltus' incoming punch, squeezing his arm as Taltus yelled in pain.

"You strike me!" Oranos yelled. "Your future master!"

Oranos slapped Taltus to the ground and double-handed him in the back, cracking the ground of the throne room. Oranos punched up Taltus by his cape, raising him over his had and throwing him across the room. Taltus slowly rose to his knees as Oranos walked toward him. No expression on his face. Just concentration.

"I am not like the Olympians you're familiar with, Taltus. I am beyond them."

"Yet, you actions prove you're no different than Zeus. Just another pathetic ruler."

"If that were so, you would be given a chance to join me. But, that is out of the question. The only thing I require of you now is your death. By my hands."

Back outside of the throne room, Thrudhawk was defeated, his head bleeding out from the broken horn. The last few ophfiends were taken down by Theus and Nano Man. Dominix was the last one standing as he was charged by the heroes. Fighting his way out of their surroundings. The Beast lunged toward Dominix, pummeling him in the face as the heroes charged up and blasted Dominix to the point of defeat.

"Seems we're done here." Norland said, catching his breath.

"We need to regroup with Taltus." Swordman said. "Let's get moving."

In the throne room, Taltus is being used like a rag doll by Oranos. Being dragged by his cape and slammed throughout the room. Oranos grabbed Taltus' head and smashed it against the wall as lava fell over his face. Taltus screamed, shoving himself from the wall, getting a punch across Oranos' face. Oranos chuckled before he punched Taltus and stomped his head into the floor. Turning his heel over Taltus' head, Oranos laughed.

"Something isn't it. To find yourself in a place where you did not understand. Your true place. Under those who are superior to you and your kind."

Taltus used both his feet, kicking Oranos in the stomach, raising himself up and charging the Blacholian god with every possible blow he could contact. Oranos stumbled in his place as Taltus went for another blow, only for Oranos to catch this one and head butt the titagod before snatching him by his throat and slamming him into the floor. Taltus caught his breath after the fall and Oranos raised his foot, stomping Taltus in the chest. Continually stomping Taltus as blood started to fly from his mouth, fueling Oranos even more as the heroes entered the room, seeing Taltus bleeding from the mouth and Oranos stomping him. The Beast saw the incident and charged against Oranos, tackling him against he lava, which fell on Beasts hand and he pulled it away, holding it from the burning. Oranos shook his head before punching the Beast and pushing him back. He looked out, seeing the heroes standing before him. He looked down toward Taltus. Beaten and barely moving. He stomped his chest once more, provoking the heroes' anger toward him. He fed off it and wanted more.

"You all came to aid your ally." Oranos said. "Now, what will you do if he dies by your delay?"

"He's not dying this day." Theus said. "I know of your kind. Dark Gods. I am familiar with them back on Eragard. You will not achieve victory."

"Ah. An Eragardian in my midst. Quaint of this day. First a titagod. Now, an Eragardian. I assume Eden has no knowledge of your presence here."

"I am here to aid my friends."

"Friends? Is that what you call them? Humans. Titagods. You consider them friends? Pathetic."

"What's with all the insults, man." Voltage said. "Show some respect."

Swordman raised his sword as Oranos measured it. Its glistening glow caught his focus.

"You wield the sword of the ancients."

"I do."

"You believe it can take me down?"

"We'll find out this day won't we."

Oranos laughed.

"We shall see."

Fortune clapped his hands as the magic formed around them. Oranos nodded.

"A sorcerer as well."

"Supreme Enchanter." Fortune replied.

"Such ancient titles do not trouble me. I was around before

there was a Supreme Enchanter and I will be here when the last Supreme Enchanter is dead."

The heroes were prepared. Another door in the throne room opened and Oranos turned. Seeing who walked out immediately caught the attention of Theus. Oranos saw the anger on his face and smiled.

"I knew she would get a reaction out of you. She came here because she knew of your task."

"Hadi." Theus said.

"Who's Hadi?" Nano Man asked.

"She's the Millennium Goddess of Death. She wants to rule all the fifteen realms in utter darkness and decay."

Hadi stood tall over the heroes, near the height of Oranos. The two dark gods showed signs of respect to each other as they stood side-by-side facing the heroes. Taltus was still on the ground, nearly encodings and coughing up blood.

"This is what you wanted," Oranos said. "Save your titagod friend and stop my invasion. Now is the time."

The heroes were ready as Hadi conjured up a spear from fire in her hands to Oranos' eyes and hands glowing with negonic energy. The battle has begun.

▼

THE IMPERATIVE ENCOUNTER

Theus screamed, streaking as lightning toward Hadi, smashing her into the lava walls as Fortune spawned three mystical whips, grabbing Oranos by his arms and neck. Voltage and Nano Man moved around the Blacholian god, firing their own attacks. Oranos grinned, pulling Fortune closer and swinging him in the air, colliding with Voltage and Nano Man. Kular attacked Oranos with his trident as Swordman jumped on the back of Oranos, pummeling him in his neck. Oranos grabbed Swordman by his head, tossing him to the floor. Norland ran through the heroes, jumping into the air and uppercuts Oranos. He stumbled as Norland continued attacking before letting out a large blast of ice lightning. The ground froze from the attack and Oranos slipped in his steps. He glanced down and shot the ground, melting the ice.

"Blizzard's power will not prevail here."

"How do you know about him?" Norland wondered.

"I know them all."

Theus and Hadi fought above them. Hammer against spear. Theus shoved Hadi and smashed her into the wall as more lava covered her upper body. Theus rushed against Hadi's chest, holding his hammer on her neck.

"Did Noldar send you?"

"I came here on my own accord. To help my brethren."

"Oranos is your brethren?"

"All Dark Gods are related. We stand to achieve the same goal."

"Not this day."

"More threats."

Hadi reversed the hold, turning Theus against the wall and holding his face against the magma. Lightning conjured up on Theus' right hand and he turned around quickly, punching Hadi across the room as he body was surrounded by his lightning. Theus spears Hadi through the wall with his power and hammer in the forefront. They rushed through the molten concrete, returning to the entry point of the castle. Below them, Dagard walked through the cracked window, holding his abdomen from the pain, gazing up to the two gods. Dagard turned his focus toward the throne room, making his way to the doors.

Oranos snatched Nano Man from the air as he flew around him, squeezing his helmet. The suit began to malfunction until Swordman jumped up, swiping his sword across Oranos' arm. Dropping Nano Man to the floor, Oranos looked at his arm, seeing the blood rising. He grinned, turning toward Swordman, nodding toward the sword.

"You're one of them."

"I am."

"Dyclos told me of you."

"Did he? Where did he run off to?"

"You'll see him again. If you survive this battle."

Fortune moved over Swordman to attack Oranos, trapping him in place with runes. Oranos recognized the symbols and struggled to pull his legs up from the ground. Fortune hovered in front of him, his hands steady as his fingers twirled.

"This is over, Oranos." Fortune proclaimed. "We have won this battle."

"You think this will stop me?!"

Voltage moved over toward Nano Man, seeing the helmet

cracked and the suit beaten. Voltage rubbed his hands together as sparks flew from them. Nathan rose, removing the helmet from his head, seeing Voltage bringing together his electricity.

"What are you doing?"

"I'm restoring your energy. Give me a second."

Voltage extended his hands as the electricity flowed in front of him like spider webs. Voltage waved the electricity over Nano Man, falling onto the suit and instantly, the suit charged up and the cracks were sealed. Nathan nodded as he learned Voltage used his own power to restore his armor.

"Thanks."

"Now, let's kick this guy's ass and go home."

"Fair point."

Oranos continued pulling himself from Fortune's trap as he was attacked on all sides by the heroes. Taltus, still on the ground began to move. Taltus raised up slowly, wiping the blood from his mouth. The door sounded, getting his attention as he saw Dagard entering with a dagger in his hand. Dagard looked toward Oranos, seeing him surrounded. He spotted Voltage and ran toward him. Taltus rose up from the ground, hovering as he flew and speared Dagard through the wall with the strength he had left. Getting the others' attention, Taltus walked through the hole as the magma fell over him. Taltus returned to the throne room and collapsed on the floor. He was burnout and his energy was gone.

"Taltus." Swordman said, rushing over to help him.

Oranos saw Taltus and grinned. Balling both his fists and pulling his arms together, Fortune noticed his movements and held the trap more tightly. Oranos screamed as he broke through the trap, shoving Fortune across the throne room. Oranos looked around at the heroes with his eyes glowing.

"This is the end."

The Beast returned into the battle, spearing Oranos and pummeling him once again. Oranos held his arms up, blocking the blows. He grabbed the Beast by his hair, head butting him and kicking him in the knees. Kular jumped up, crashing into reground, causing a shockwave of energy to impact Oranos. Oranos walked through the wave and backhanded Kular into the wall.

"I got him!" Voltage yelled.

Voltage moved forward, making his body phase as Oranos went in for an attack. He turned himself around, expanding his power around Oranos, electricity him at every move. Fortune rushed in and reformed the trap around Oranos' legs and his arms. From above, Theus returned to the room, giving the heroes the impression that Hadi was defeated. Theus flew over toward Fortune and let out a large blast of lightning against Oranos. Kular stood up, twirling the trident, forming a whirlwind around Oranos. Norland ran in and let out his own lightning to attack Oranos. Nano Man hovered above Oranos and unleashed a blast of the ultrabeam atop Oranos' head. The Blacholian god was surrounded at every corner. The heroes' continued their attacks, believing they have Oranos where they wanted him. Oranos struggled to maintain his strength against all the powers around him as he fell to one knee.

"He's down!" Voltage yelled.

"He's not finished yet." Fortune responded. "Keep going!"

Oranos fell to both knees, as his hands touched the floor. His head was hung low as the heroes continued the attacks. Swordman looked over as he helped Taltus to his feet. He saw Oranos on the ground being hit with the waves of power. Taltus rose his head, seeing Oranos on the floor. He glared closer, sensing something surging within Oranos.

"He…" Taltus said. "He's not finished."

"What do you mean?" Swordman asked.

"Tell them… Tell them to move back."

Before Swordman could let out the words, Oranos rose up to

his feet, taking the heroes by surprise and swiped his arms, blasting all of the heroes with their own attacks. They fell to the ground as Oranos stood over them, grasping his own power and holding his fists. His eyes flowed brighter than before as he grinned with a low laugh.

"You seem to have underestimated one such as I."

"No." Taltus grunted.

Oranos glared over toward Swordman and Taltus, blasting negonic energy from his eyes. Taltus pushed Swordman over as the beams impacted him. Taltus fell to the floor as Swordman rose up and ran toward Oranos. Oranos quickly moved out of his path and grabbed Swordman by his head, holding him tightly to the point he dropped the sword. Oranos slammed Swordman into the wall and tossed him across the throne room, where he fell and rolled over toward Taltus. All of the heroes were down and Oranos stood over them. Sighing at his victory. Looking around, he saw several of them slowly rising to their feet.

"Stay down!" Oranos yelled. "Save yourselves from another moment of defeat."

"No." Fortune said. "I will not stand down. Especially against those of your kind."

"As the Doctor said," Voltage said. "We won't stand down."

"Neither will I." Norland said.

"Nor I." Kular responded, slamming the trident.

"Neither am I." Nano Man said, charging up his suit.

The Beast rose up, letting out a loud roar while beating his chest. Swordman stood up, seeing his sword laying on the ground in front of Oranos. Fortune saw the sword, picking it up with his magic, moving it over to Swordman. He grabbed it and gave Fortune a nod. Theus picked himself up with a whirlwind of lighting. The lightning ceased, showing Theus healed of the wounds and his hands surging with power.

"I will not surrender!" Theus yelled.

"So, you all want to die rather than live as my servants."

"Better to die in freedom than live as slaves." Swordman responded.

Oranos nodded.

"Very well. I hope you've given your condolences to the ones you love. Because you won't be going back home to see them."

"Now, everyone!" Fortune yelled. "Hit him at once!"

The heroes returned their attacks on Oranos. Hitting him at every corner. Oranos allowed them the attacks as he stood still, grinning and relishing in the attacks. Swordman knew something was off and remembered Taltus' words. Placing the sword back into its sheath, he walked over, extending his hand.

"Wait!" Swordman yelled. "Stop the attack!"

"Why?!" Fortune asked. "We have him once more!"

"He's absorbing the energy! You're making him stronger!"

"How do you know this?"

"Taltus told me!" Now cease the attacks!"

Fortune shook his head, disagreeing.

"We can't let him win, Kenari. We can't."

"He will only win if you continue hitting him with all you have without a pure plan!"

"We have no other alternative! This is what we must do!"

"Yes!" Oranos said. "Let out all you have against me! For it is the only way to defeat one such as I."

Nano Man continued the ultra-beam, as his A.I. caught something peculiar forming in the area. He paused the beam with Fortune looking at him.

"What are you doing?!" Fortune yelled. "Hit him again!"

"Something's not right in here."

Oranos' eyes glowed again as he jumped into the air and stomped the ground, returning the attacks onto the heroes in a much greater force. Even knocking Swordman and Nano Man through the walls. The heroes were down and not moving. Taltus was still unconscious as Oranos measured his surroundings. He sensed the heroes were defeated and returned to his throne seat and sat down.

"I have won." Oranos proclaimed.

"Oranos of Blachole." said a chilling voice from the unknown.

Oranos stood up from the seat, turning back and forth to see where the voice originated from. He saw no one. The heroes were still down. Oranos continued searching as the voice spoke to him once again. Swordman slowly raised his head from the rubble, glimpsing Oranos yelling at the unseen force.

"Oranos of Blachole." The voice said again.

"Show yourself!" Oranos yelled. "Face me!"

"As you desire."

Within the throne room beamed a great light, brighter than the sun as Swordman shielded his eyes from the impact. The light even emitted a heat of its own. Oranos stared at the light, looking into it closely. The light slowly dimmed as Swordman saw Oranos staring. Swordman looked ahead, seeing a figure dressed in all white. From its cloak to its hood. Yet, its face was as dark as darkness could be and its eyes were as bright as the sun could achieve. Oranos found himself staring into the eyes of the Specter Errant.

"You." Oranos said. "This is not possible."

"Oranos of Blachole. I am the Specter Errant and you have altered something which shall not be altered."

"I am the Blacholian Dark God!" Oranos yelled. "I can alter and change anything that comes my way!"

"You cannot. For what you have done has changed the future for the worse. Now, I will correct your mistakes as they shall be erased from time itself."

"You will not!" Oranos screamed.

Oranos went for a punch, yet Specter Errant caught Oranos' fist in his own hand and punched Oranos back through the walls with the lava falling over him. Specter Errant moved his focus toward the heroes and raised his hands above them. Light emitted from his fingers and fell atop the heroes. Each of them. The light entered their foreheads, traveling throughout their body at every limb and moving toward their chest and ceasing its brightness.

"Therefore, rise." Specter Errant commanded. "Stand and fight this day."

Each of the heroes arose from the floor. Finding themselves completely rejuvenated and fully charged. Voltage let out several blasts of lightning, catching him off his guard as the moved with much greater speed than he's familiar with.

"Wow!"

They each tested out their power, revealing it in its fullness of strength. In front of them, through the rubble, Oranos arose and stepped forward, wiping the magma from his shoulders. Behind them, they could hear lighting sparking and as they turned, Taltus arose. Hovering above the ground with his eyes fixed on Oranos. The heroes stood together with Errant in the forefront.

"Together, you will defeat Oranos." Errant said. "This is your final stand."

VI

<u>THE FINAL STAND</u>

The Specter Errant led the Resistance and the Protectors against Oranos. The battle began with Oranos deflecting the lightning from Voltage, Norland, and Theus before he was attacked from above by Nano Man. Oranos snatched Nano Man from the air, throwing him into Theus. The Beast tackled Oranos once more, grabbing him by his throat and chokeslamming him. Oranos stood up, kicking the Beast from near him as he was held down by Fortune's magic. Fighting off the magic, Fortune dodged the incoming blast from Oranos' eyes. Swordman rushed toward Oranos, slashing him in the abdomen with the sword and his calves. Kular moved over, swiping the trident across Oranos' legs, causing him to fall on his back as Fortune returned the magic onto him, sealing him into the floor.

"This will not stop me."

Oranos let out a massive burst of energy, breaking the magic barrier from around him as he jumped toward Fortune, grabbing him by his throat and shoving him to the wall. Oranos grinned as he choked Fortune. Errant swiftly approached Oranos, holding him by his head and tossing him into his throne seat. Oranos looked at the throne and smirked.

"You place me in my seat?"

"Not what you are thinking." Errant said, going around the throne. "It was only a signal."

Oranos looked up, seeing Taltus hovering above him. Enraged, Oranos bolted from his seat toward the titagod, yet, only to find himself missing the attack as Taltus turned back and speared Oranos through the wall and back outside into the castle. Taltus continued the attack, taking Oranos to the front gate where they entered from the portal. Swordman looked ahead.

"We need to reach them quickly."

"Stand still." Errant said. "I will bring you to them."

Errant raised his arms and transported the heroes back to their entry spot. Seeing Taltus standing over Oranos, punching him continually before unleashing a blast of his lightning blast into Oranos' own eyes. Swordman went to assist Taltus, however, Errant held his hand up in front of him. Nodding. Swordman comprehended and sheathed his sword. Taltus continued the attacks. From punches to lighting vision and he even flew into the air and crashed down on Oranos' chest with his feet. Taltus stepped back, seeing Oranos was defeated. The Blacholian god struggled to stand.

"The fight has been won." Errant said. "All is returned to as planned."

"Planned?" Fortune asked. "What are you not telling us, spirit?"

"I believe Oranos knows what I speak of." Errant said, turning toward Oranos.

Oranos raised himself up, holding his chest and rubbing his eyes.

"This was an unfair battle." Oranos stated. "I had you all defeated. I won. Yet, this spirit proceeded to aid you to defer your deaths. This will not stand."

"Don't hold it highly, Oranos. This is only the beginning of something greater."

"I will hear no more of this."

Taltus went to attack Oranos and was stopped by Errant. The

battle was over as Oranos leaned against the gated walls. Theus looked around at the area.

"Where's Hadi?" Theus asked. "I left her here after I defeated her."

"She has returned to her own realm." Errant answered. "Do not concern your mind on her whereabouts."

"Leave my domain." Oranos commanded. "Leave Blachole!"

Errant nodded, opening a larger portal. The heroes took their leave with Taltus being last. He turned toward Oranos as his eyes sparked.

"If you return to Earth once again, it will be your last."

"I'm counting on it, titagod."

The portal closed with Oranos returning to his castle, holding himself from the pain.

Returning the heroes back onto the streets of Newark where they last stood, Swordman looked at Errant's attire, seeing the same mark on his chest.

"Was this one of the matters you warned me about?" Kular asked.

"One. Yes." Errant replied. "In a small matter."

"I see you have questions."

"You bear the same mark." Swordman said.

"I do."

"You worked for Oranos?" Taltus asked. "Why wear his mark?"

"This is not Oranos' mark. It is the Mark of Helven."

"Helven?" Voltage asked.

"A realm far from this place. Far from many. The mark does not belong to Oranos. It belongs to-"

"Negiter." Swordman answered.

"Correct." Errand said.

"How do you know?" Taltus wondered.

"Because he was the one behind the Battle of Retropolis."

"And where is this Negiter?" Fortune questioned.

"Trapped." Errant answered. "You have no need to worry about him. Much is still yet to happen."

"Happen?" Taltus said. "What else is there that we don't know?"

"You will all know in time. For now, return to your own estates. Settle the disputes in your areas and do what you were made to do. When the other circumstances arrive, you will know what must be done."

Errant hovered above them as the bright light returned.

"We will meet again."

Specter Errant vanished in the light as the Resistance and Protectors each returned to their own respective places. Later in the day, Kenari spoke with his wife, Allison who told him of the details regarding Harold Hunt's plans. Kenari took her words as he entered the sword lair. While inside, he pulled out a folder from the archives, detailed on the Enforcement Order and its members.

EPILOGUE

Kex Kendrick sat inside an office with Marion von Eldric opposite of him. On the table were two separate files. From the doors entered several V.A.U.L.T. guards. They stood against the wall as a visitor entered the office. Kex stood up, clapping his hands.

"Good. You've arrived."

Standing in front of them was Maveth, The Death-Bringer. He sat attestable opposite of Marion, removing his helmet. Kex handed him the two files and he opened them both. Within the files were detailed plans and photos of The Swordman and Taltus.

"I know when we last spoke, you chose your prize in hunting down The Swordman. However, as a favor from a true supporter, I am giving you the details to take down the titagod."

"I understand." Maveth said. "Yet, The Swordman is my first priority."

"I get it."

From the doors arrived both A.B. and Gage Hark, surprising the three at the table. A.B. saw Maveth and nodded with a smirk.

"I wasn't aware the Death-Bringer would be here as well."

"On business, Adrian. As I always am."

Gage handed A.B. a file pf their own. A.B. slid the file in the middle of the table. Kex grabbed it and looked. He nodded before handing it over to Marion who handed it to Maveth.

"Before you deal with the Swordman and this titagod,

Maveth. I would like to see what my team is capable of against these Resistance."

"You want to test your team to the fully potential." Kex said. "This is even greater than I could've thought out."

Maveth nodded.

"Very well then. I will allow your Enforcement Order to face the Resistance. See what they're capable of. Afterwards, if The Swordman is still alive, I will deal with him myself."

"Do what you must, Danton." A.B. said. "All I need to know is if these risen heroes are as powerful as the people proclaim them to be."

"Oh. They are." A soft voice echoed from the door.

Getting their attention, they turned to the door to see Death herself walking into the office. She smiled at them as she clapped her hands.

"Death." Kex said.

"Nice to see you again. Good to see all of you as well. For the first time."

"I have my team fixing your mistakes across the world." A.B. said.

"I know. But, don't fret. It's all for a good cause."

"How so?" Kex asked.

"Because as you all have plans for these heroes, I have something specially for The Swordman. If Maveth doesn't end him."

"Oh, I will end him. It is my purpose."

"Ha! We'll see."

NEXT BOOK IN

THE DARK TITAN UNIVERSE SAGA....

UNDERWORLD

A BOOK RETURNING TO THE SCATTERED HEROES ACROSS THE DARK TITAN UNIVERSE. INCLUDING THE RETURNS OF THE EAST COAST ALLIANCE, ATOM-ZERO, AND THE DEVIL-KNIGHT.

ABOUT THE AUTHOR

Ty'Ron W. C. Robinson II is the author of several works of fiction. Including the *Dark Titan Universe Saga*, *The Haunted City Saga*, EverWar Universe, Symbolum Venatores, Frightened!, Instincts, and others. More information pertaining to the author and stories can be found at darktitanentertainment.com.

Twitter: @TyronRobinsonII

Twitter: @DarkTitan_
Instagram: @darktitanentertainment
Facebook: @DarkTitanEnt
Pinterest: @darktitanentertainment
YouTube: Dark Titan Entertainment